BY THE AUTHOR OF *THE ZOMBIE CHASERS*
JOHN KLOEPFER

ILLUSTRATED BY
NICK EDWARDS

HARPER
An Imprint of HarperCollinsPublishers

Galaxy's Most Wanted

Copyright © 2014 by Alloy Entertainment and John Kloepfer

All rights reserved. Printed in the United States of America.

No part of this book may be used or reproduced in any manner whatsoever without written permission except in the case of brief quotations embodied in critical articles and reviews. For information address HarperCollins Children's Books, a division of HarperCollins Publishers, 10 East 53rd Street, New York, NY 10022..

www.harpercollinschildrens.com

Library of Congress Cataloging-in-Publication Data

Kloepfer, John.

Galaxy's most wanted / John Kloepfer ; illustrated by Nick Edwards. — First edition.

pages   cm

Summary: "When thirteen-year-old Kevin Brewer and his camp buddies summon an alien to earth, they know they'll win a blue ribbon in the science competition—but they don't expect to find themselves in the middle of an interstellar war"—Provided by publisher.

ISBN 978-0-06-223101-7 (hardback)

[1. Extraterrestrial beings—Fiction.   2. Camps—Fiction.
3. Science fiction.   4. Humorous stories.   5. Youth's art.]
I. Edwards, Nick, date, illustrator.   II. Title.

PZ7.K6845Gal   2014   2013047945

[Fic]—dc23   CIP

                                                                          AC

Typography by Ray Shappell

14 15 16 17 18   CG/RRDH   10 9 8 7 6 5 4 3 2 1

❖

First Edition

For Nonny

The darkness swept in as another day of summer camp came to a close. It had been a fairly ordinary day, but this was no ordinary sleepover camp. Northwest Horizons was the best STEM camp in America—science, technology, engineering, and math. The kids who attended Northwest Horizons all had one thing in common. They all dreamed of being the next big thing—making groundbreaking discoveries, starting their own companies, and one day becoming billionaires. Most would probably wind up as kooky college professors; however, there was always someone who might make it big. And at this particular camp, there were at least a few who could do it.

Kevin Brewer was one such camper. He was interested in everything: physics, biology, and chemistry. Plus, he was good at math. Kevin particularly loved robotics, making machines move on their own and one day maybe even think on their own. But right now Kevin's only concern was winning the Invention Convention, the most prestigious competition at science camp, and beating Alexander Russ, his nemesis four years and counting.

There was no way Kevin was going to come in second this year, as he had every single other summer, because this year the winners of the NWH Invention Convention received the best prize ever: an automatic spot in the International Science Competition in Honolulu. The winning team would get to fly to Hawaii and compete against kids from all over the world. And if they won first place, they got to ride into outer space on a NASA shuttle with real astronauts.

Kevin stood at the edge of the woods dressed in dark jeans and a black hoodie, trying to blend in with the night. Curfew was less than an hour away. He had to make this quick.

"Ready?" Kevin asked, turning to three of his close friends—Warner Reed, Tara Swift, and TJ Boyd—each of them wearing similar all-black camouflage.

Tara Swift peered over the top of Kevin's head, her thick black-rimmed eyeglasses teetering on the edge of her nose. Tara was slightly taller than Kevin and the other boys, and she wore her dark, curly hair pulled up into pigtails. Aside from Warner, Kevin's best friend, Tara was Kevin's favorite person at camp. Not only was she supersmart and great at building things out of next to nothing, but she was also pretty cool just to hang out with. "Are you sure this is a good idea?" she asked him.

"No, it's not," said Warner. "This is pointless!" Despite the fact that Warner was one of the smartest kids at camp, he didn't care much about science and definitely not about the Invention Convention. All he really wanted to do was play video games, read comic books, and watch horror movies. The only reason he said he came to camp was because his parents wanted him out of the house, but Kevin knew that deep down, Warner really did like it here.

"Come on, guys," said Kevin. "The Invention Convention's less than a week away, and we've got diddly-squat."

Up until now, they had spent almost the entire summer trying to design a computer program that could do a person's homework, but when they asked it to write an essay on photosynthesis, all they got was a rambling five hundred words on the history of photography and the electronic synthesizer. TJ attempted to reprogram the software, but in the end it was more frustrating to use the homework machine than it was to do the actual homework assignment. Kevin knew they'd need something better than an A+ paper to beat Alexander anyway.

"Kevin," Warner said, sighing in defeat. "You've been coming to this nerd camp longer than anyone. You should know by now that Alexander Russ is never going to lose, so why don't we just build a baking-soda volcano and call it a day?"

Kevin took a deep breath. "We can't give up. If we

can just figure out what Alexander and his chumps are working on, we might have a real chance of taking them down." Besides being a jerk, and rubbing his winning streak in Kevin's face, Alexander was a liar and a cheat. Alexander's father owned a successful technology company, and he had no problem "helping" his only son win the Invention Convention every year. A little too much help, if Kevin had anything to say about it.

TJ nodded his head in agreement. He wasn't much of a talker. Word around the campfire was that he'd damaged his voice box in a botched robotics experiment, but Kevin knew that was only gossip. He had gone to school with TJ since the first grade. He'd always been pretty quiet, although he would speak up in class when he had to. But when he showed up at camp, he kept completely and utterly mum. The truth was that nobody knew why TJ had suddenly decided to stop talking except for TJ, and he wasn't telling.

"Okay dum-dums," Tara said, staring into the forest's black depths. "If we're gonna do this, let's do it. Who's going first?" She tapped her nose and said, "Not it." Quickly, Warner and TJ touched the tips of their noses before Kevin even knew what was happening. "Kevin's it," they all jinxed each other. Kevin didn't much care, though. He wanted to be first.

"Okay, follow me," Kevin whispered, waving them along as he crept into the dark woods. A warm breeze rustled the leaves and a lone owl hooted from the treetops as Kevin and his friends approached a clearing in the middle of the forest.

Kevin snuck behind an evergreen and hid out of

sight. Warner, TJ, and Tara spread out and took cover behind trees of their own. Kevin was trying hard to breathe quietly in and out. He could hear his own heartbeat thumping in his chest. Slowly, he peered out around the tree trunk.

There they were.

Two figures were lit up in a soft glowing light. Kevin recognized the silhouettes as Luke and Dante, Alexander's teammates. Behind them a saucer-shaped vessel levitated three, and then five, and then ten feet off the ground.

Someone was riding it. Dirt and leaves spiraled upward as a *whoosh* of air blasted out from underneath.

Kevin made eye contact with Warner, whose eyes bulged with amazement. Warner pointed toward the saucer and mouthed the word: *Awesomeness.*

So this was what they were up against. Alexander's team, the Vainglorious Math Nerds, had built a freakin' hovercraft. Kevin's stomach churned with the beginnings of an ulcer.

The hovercraft descended, carrying the VMN's

pint-size leader, and powered down with a mechanical sigh. Alexander the Great jumped to the ground from his high-tech chariot, hooting and high-fiving his teammates. The three boys proceeded to bump chests and howl like wild orangutans.

This was going to be tougher than Kevin had thought. He signaled his team to head back so they could regroup, and TJ, Tara, and then Warner crept away silently, disappearing into the shadows. Kevin was about to tiptoe off, too, when his footstep startled a nearby squirrel. In a flash, the skittish fur ball bolted up into the treetops in a loud flurry of leaves.

Uh-oh. Kevin gasped and his chest tightened.

Alexander swung his flashlight toward the noise. "Who goes there?" he called out with the authority of a king.

Kevin stood stone-still behind the tree. His pulse quickened as the voices drew closer. Their high-beam flashlights cut through the darkness like lightsabers.

Kevin sucked in his belly and held his breath as long as he dared, then exhaled soundlessly.

"Who's they-er?" Luke called out in a playful yet sinister tone.

Kevin wanted to run, but couldn't find the guts to move. They were way too close. Three against one. He didn't like the odds.

"Come out, come out, whoever you are . . . ," Dante sang.

"It's 'come out, *wherever* you are,'" Alexander corrected him. "Not *whoever*, stupid."

"But we don't know *who* it is, either," said Dante.

Alexander flicked his teammate's earlobe hard, and Kevin took off running.

"There! Get him!" Alexander yelled as he whipped his head around and tagged Kevin with his flashlight. "The little snoop's getting away!"

Kevin had a nice head start, but when it came to running, he had only one gear, and that was slow. Luke and Dante charged through the pinewoods and were gaining on him fast.

Kevin faked right and broke left, pushing through

a low-hanging tree branch as if it were a turnstile. *Thwack!* The branch snapped back, nailing Luke in the gut as Kevin sprinted off. Luke doubled over and fell to the ground, tripping up Dante, who flew face-first into a pricker bush.

"Yow!" Dante's painful yelps echoed into the treetops.

Kevin raced out of the forest, heading back to his cabin. He rounded the lake, glittering peacefully in the moonlight, and slowed his pace once he was in the clear. He stopped behind a bunkhouse and looked over his shoulder. Still nobody in sight. Kevin wheezed, trying to catch his breath. He reached into his camp-issued fanny pack and pulled out his inhaler.

Kevin closed his eyes, about to take a puff, when he felt a pudgy hand come down on his shoulder.

"Hey, Kevo," Alexander said, snatching the inhaler out of Kevin's grasp. "You don't mind if I call you Kevo, do you, Kevo?"

"Give it back," Kevin wheezed. "I need it!" The asthma burned in Kevin's chest, making him feel as though he were sucking in air through a narrow straw.

"You think you can just spy on my team and get away with it?" Alexander tossed the inhaler from one hand to the other with a glint of evil in his eyes.

Kevin lunged forward, but Alexander dodged his swiping arms and spun out of reach. The alpha nerd danced around, taunting Kevin. "Ooh, I'm Kevin," he said. "And I don't breathe good."

Kevin could hear Tara and Warner both calling his name from the woods, but he couldn't yell back. Kevin lunged at Alexander again, this time pushing him hard enough to make him stumble backward. A gooey *squish* sounded underneath the bully's foot, and Alexander's eyes went bright and fierce, his nostrils flaring as he sniffed what was now on the bottom of his shoe.

"You got goose poop on my shoe!" Alexander roared.

"I can't breathe!" Kevin tried to shout, but his voice came out only in a squeaky whisper.

"Hey!" a girl's voice yelled from behind them as Tara stuck her head around the corner of the cabin. "Give him the inhaler, Alexander! You're gonna give him brain damage!"

"Like anyone would notice." Alexander laughed at his own smart remark.

"Give it back, dorkweed." Warner appeared from the edge of the woods. "Or you can kiss your precious late-night Snickers stash good-bye," he threatened. It was a well-known fact among the campers that Warner was the man to see about a two a.m. sugar craving. They paid top dollar for access to Warner's junk-food supply, and Alexander was no different.

"You wouldn't dare cut me off," Alexander sneered. "I'm your best customer."

"Oh, but I would," Warner said, cracking his knuckles. "Now hand over the inhaler."

Alexander narrowed his eyes, staring at Kevin, Warner, and Tara. "All right," he said with a smirk, and then proceeded to scrape the goose poop off the sole of his sneaker with the mouthpiece of Kevin's inhaler. "New flavor," he cackled, tossing it at Kevin's

feet. "Just for you, Kevo. . . ."

"You little—" Warner charged after Alexander, who darted back to his own cabin, almost tripping over his own feet.

Tara jumped in front of Warner and held him back. "Don't do it, Warner. He's not worth it!"

Kevin dropped to his knees and grabbed the inhaler off the ground in a hurry. He wiped it off as best as he could on his T-shirt, and then shook it, bracing himself for the wretched flavor. He had no choice. His friends all watched in horror as he took a quick puff, holding the medicine in his lungs. Kevin gagged and coughed. The taste was terrible, but at least the asthma attack was over.

"Thanks, man," said Kevin to Warner once he could breathe again.

"Please," Warner replied as he helped Kevin to his feet. "I eat nerds like him for breakfast." He pulled out a box of Nerds candy and poured an avalanche of red pebbles into his mouth.

Kevin walked up the steps of the cabin, where he, Warner, and TJ were all bunking in the same room for the summer, and stomped straight to the bathroom to rinse out his mouth. The bunkhouse was split up into five separate bedrooms, which each housed three to four campers at a time. There was a single room for the counselor and a large bathroom, and they all shared a common room off the hallway.

When Kevin returned from the bathroom, Bailey, their counselor, was talking to Warner, TJ, and Tara in the common room. Bailey was tall and skinny with a pointy nose and a shaggy blond mop of hair, which he was constantly pushing out of his eyes. Kevin always wondered why their counselor didn't just get himself a haircut.

"Hey, Kev," Bailey said, flicking his blond locks. "Everything okay?"

"Uh-huh," Kevin lied, still tasting the rancid flavor on his tongue. He knew he should have told on Alexander, but Kevin was no tattletale.

Bailey looked at his watch. "Almost time for bed, guys," he said. "Tara, you should get going back to your bunk."

"Wait, we need to have a quick team meeting first," Kevin said. "Secret IC stuff," he added, sensing that their counselor might try and stick around.

Bailey looked at the time again and furrowed his eyebrows. "Okay, but make it quick. You only have about ten minutes," he said, and then left them alone to talk.

"Dude," Warner said as the team gathered on the couch. "Alexander really crossed a line. That was the nastiest thing I've ever seen."

"You're telling me," Kevin said. "That was the grossest thing I've ever tasted!"

"Alexander," Tara grumbled, looking at Kevin.

"He's got to be stopped. We have to take him down at the convention."

"That hovercraft he's got is gonna be tough to beat, but we just have to think bigger than him," Kevin said, and TJ nodded enthusiastically.

"If I'm in, it's to teach that twerp a lesson," Warner said, flipping open an issue of his favorite comic book.

"Well, we better think fast." Tara yawned. "I need to get back before I get in trouble."

"Okay, okay," said Kevin. "What about—no, not that," he thought out loud. "Or how about a—nah, that's no good either!" His mind was reeling. All they needed was one great idea, but he couldn't think of a single thing better than Alexander's hovercraft. He gritted his teeth and growled involuntarily while TJ just sat there silently, scratching his head.

The crickets chirping outside rose in volume as Warner crunched some more Nerds and read his comic. Kevin glared at his buddy, a little annoyed that he wasn't helping. A few moments later, Warner abruptly closed the cover and looked up with a satisfied smirk on his face. "Brainstorm," he said.

"That's what we're doing," Tara snapped with her chin resting on her fist.

"No, dummy!" Warner said, now holding up the comic book and pointing to the title, which read "*Brainstorm* by Max Greyson." "Take a look at this," he said, and flipped to a page in the middle that showed a drawing of some futuristic-looking high-tech gizmo.

"What the heck is that?" asked Kevin.

"That, my friend," said Warner, "is a galactascope."

"What's a galactascope?" Tara sounded skeptical.

"Well, *Tara*," Warner began. "A galactascope is—well, it's basically an instant messenger across the entire galaxy."

"But that's impossible," Kevin argued.

"Because you can't send messages faster than the speed of light. It totally violates Einstein's theory of relativity," Tara piped in.

"She's right, Warner." Kevin shrugged. "This has to be real science, not some half-baked comic-book mumbo jumbo."

"Guys, I'm serious," Warner said. "I can't believe I hadn't thought of this already. This is the real thing. The author, Max Greyson, was abducted by aliens at the age of twenty-three. Like, way back in the eighties. He's ancient now. But he went from being a simple-minded police officer to a cult comic-book author in the years following his abduction. There's even been speculation that the devices described in his work are actual alien technology that was downloaded into his brain."

"Ha!" Tara scoffed. "What a load of hooey!"

"Just take a look. It's all here." Warner handed Kevin the comic.

Kevin studied the description from the captions, squinting his eyes at the illustrations. TJ leaned over Kevin's shoulder, checking out the diagram and blue-prints laid out on the comic book's glossy pages.

When Kevin broke the galactascope down into its basic parts, he saw that it could actually be built. They could probably even get most of the stuff they needed from the scrap room down at the robotics workshop. *There's no way it's gonna work, though,* he thought. It

violated almost every law of physics. But if they were going to have any chance of claiming first prize, then that's exactly what needed to happen.

Kevin looked up from the comic book. "Okay, let's do it."

Kevin woke to the sound of the breakfast bell dinging in the distance. He wiped crusts of sleep from the corners of his eyes, put on his glasses, and took a double puff of his inhaler. He dropped down from the top bunk and scanned the room. Warner hadn't even made it to bed. He slept soundly on the floor surrounded by half-empty bags of chips spilling every which way. At least two dozen open DVDs were splayed out in front of him, and there were candy wrappers all over the place, mostly Kit Kats, Kevin and Warner's favorite candy bar.

TJ was up and out of the room already but had left a note at the foot Kevin's bed.

Dear Slackers,

When you're not so busy snoozing, get the following supplies and meet me and Tara for breakfast.

A metal rolling cart

An HD digital satellite dish

One 1-inch-thick piece of pyrite—that's fool's gold, Warner.

One amethyst crystal

One handheld laser signaling device

A small backup generator

Three car batteries

Four heavy-duty extension cords

Three USB hookups

One rabbit's foot, for luck. We're gonna need it.

Check you later,

TJ

P.S. Tara says you both better bring your A games.

P.P.S. Especially you, Warner!

"I guess these guys got an early start," Kevin said aloud after reading through the list. He nudged Warner with his foot. "Wake up, man."

Warner stirred and rolled over. "Just give me five more minutes," he said, groggy-eyed, before flopping over and going back to sleep.

"Come on, buddy, let's get this show on the road," Kevin said, but his friend kept snoozing. "Warner!"

Once Kevin finally woke up his sleepy-headed pal, the boys got dressed quickly and hustled out of the bunkhouse. Strolling through the sunshine, they walked briskly across the main lawn toward the long,

rectangular science lab trailers parked behind the mess hall.

Northwest Horizons was nestled in the lush forests of Oregon along the eastern bank of a small, deep lake where a few of the younger campers were already collecting silt samples before their morning ecology lab. The large white trailers didn't look like much, though enclosed within them were some of the most state-of-the-art scientific facilities in all of the Pacific Northwest. But the crown jewel of the camp was the

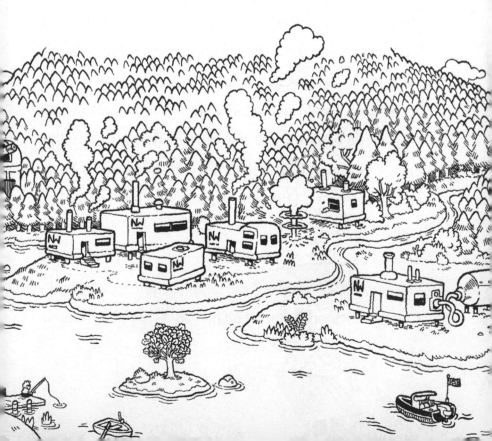

Russ Planetarium and Observatory, where mind-bending astronomy labs and guest lectures were held. Like at any good camp, though, physical activity was encouraged. There was a field house with a gymnasium, but it was mostly used as a robot-versus-robot battleground.

Kevin and Warner made their way to the scrap room, a trailer between the robotics and forensics labs.

"Jackpot," Kevin said, tapping all ten of his fingertips together like a mad scientist, happy to find a fully stocked room without any other campers searching for last-minute parts. Kevin and Warner immediately started rummaging through the bins of electronics and appliances. Kevin unloaded a bunch of circuit boards off a metal rolling cart, and Warner dug up a satellite dish, a tangle of USB and extension cords, and a laser-signaling device. They also found a small generator and two out of the three car batteries.

"Looks like we got pretty much everything, Kev," Warner said, loading their parts onto an unused cart in the corner. He wiped the sweat off his brow. "Let's hit the mess hall before we stop by the geology lab. I'm stizz-arving!"

"Me too, man," Kevin said. "I hope they still have some of those raspberry Danishes left."

"I call last raspberry Danish!" Warner blurted out as if by reflex.

"No way, man," Kevin said. "I totally just called it!" Not taking any chances, he ran out the door.

The cart full of supplies rattled and clanked as Kevin and Warner rolled into the cafeteria. At the far table, over by the breakfast buffet, the Vainglorious Math Nerds—Alexander, Luke, and Dante—turned in their chairs, eyeing the boys' goods. Trying to ward off any would-be snoopers, Kevin had covered it with a spare bedsheet from their room. This way no one could hazard a guess about their new project.

"What took you guys so long?" Tara looked up from the table for a second before going back to work. She was drawing up a rough blueprint for their design. The *Brainstorm* comic book was creased open in front of her, and the morning sun gleamed off the glossy pages.

"Hey, you gotta be careful with that," said Warner, picking up his comic book. "This is a limited edition."

"If you don't put that back down," Tara said, *"you're* gonna be a limited edition."

TJ peered silently at the galactascope diagram, holding a magnifying glass up to his right eyeball, then jotted down some notes they would need for the instant messaging program code. TJ was something of a computer-programming prodigy, which was why Kevin had convinced TJ that this was the summer camp for him.

"How long do you think it will take you to write

the code?" Tara asked TJ.

TJ held up two fingers, then a third.

"Two or three hours," Kevin confirmed for Tara, knowing TJ's signals.

"Where are we going to build this thing?" Warner said, chewing a spoonful of cereal with his mouth open.

"What about the old sports shed?" Kevin said.

"Great idea, man." Warner swallowed his food. "That's the last place anyone goes around here."

"Before we head over," Kevin said, "let me just . . . we're gonna want a detailed record of this." He took out a fresh camp-issued logbook and flipped it open to the first page:

Project: G-Scope
Mission: Contact alien life (!)
Location: Northwest Horizons Science Camp
Date: 22 June 2014

From the logbook of Kevin Brewer:
9:05 a.m.: Arrive at sports shed, set up shop.

9:15 a.m.: This place = crawling with spiders! Warner keeps tickling back of my arm so that I think a spider's crawling on me. Note: get fake rubber snake to put in his bed.

10:00 a.m.: Energy source installed on lower shelf of cart.

11:00 a.m.: TJ finishes galactascope operating system; uploads the file to Warner's PS3. System is a go!

12:30 p.m.: Lunch break. Fingers crossed for chicken tenders and french fries.

Much to their delight, Kevin, Warner, Tara, and TJ all returned to the sports shed with their bellies filled with chicken fingers and curly fries. Now they were ready to get back to work. And they had a lot of it. The galactascope was nowhere close to being done.

"All right, guys!" Kevin said, closing the door behind them. "Time to finish this bad boy."

In a few hours' time, Warner finished installing the

laser device to reflect off the pyrite, and Tara worked some mechanical magic so that the satellite dish could be wired through the computer system.

"Okay," Tara said. She set down a screwdriver and lifted her safety goggles to wipe the sweat from her forehead. "I think we can finally turn this baby on."

Kevin noted the time in his log, then took a deep breath as Warner pulled the rip cord on the generator. The galactascope revved up, then grumbled and sputtered out. He pulled it again.

"Dude, give it a sec," Kevin said. "You're gonna brea—" Warner yanked the cord once more and the generator suddenly powered on, silencing Kevin midspeech.

"See, it's *fine*," said Warner, pointing to their device, which was rumbling loudly. A few seconds later, the computer inputs started to spark, and smoke began to rise out of the PS3 console.

"Uh-oh," Kevin murmured as the top of the galactascope ignited with a small blue-orange flame. Tara sprinted over by the door to the shed and snatched the emergency fire extinguisher off the wall.

"Look out, boys!" She aimed the nozzle at their invention and doused Warner's PS3 in white foam.

"My PlayStation!" Warner cried.

"Chill out, man," said Tara. "You've got a PS4, don't you?"

"Yeah, he does," Kevin said. "And we're going to need it."

"No way! Dude, Kev, you know I love you, man, but come on—that's my pride and joy," Warner pleaded.

"Warner!" Tara pointed the fire extinguisher at his midsection. "I'm beginning to doubt your commitment to this team."

By the time Warner agreed to give up his prized possession and Kevin had rewired a new generator from the robotics lab, it was long past dinnertime. Luckily, their hard work had paid off. The new generator growled and chugged and then started to hum. They inspected the new galactascope setup for any signs of shorting out, but everything looked stable.

"We did it," Kevin said, half in shock. "It works!"

"Now for the finishing touches," Tara spoke as she began painting a team logo on the side of the rolling cart with the words "The ETs' Galactascope."

"Who are the ETs?" Warner asked, making a face.

"We are," Tara said. "The Extraordinary Terrestrials."

"Wait, I already gave us a name," Warner said. "I thought we were calling ourselves the Little Pascals?"

"We were," said Tara. "Which is why I had to think of a new name."

"I love it," Kevin said. "Did you just make that up?"

"Yup," Tara said. "Coming up with awesome names is kinda my thing. I'm in this all-girl punk band back home. Haven't I mentioned it? Polly and the Peptides. I came up with that, too. Anyway—" Tara focused on her paintbrush and finished the little *e* at the end of the word "galactascope." Then she quickly painted an Earthlike planet getting bombarded with radio signals from outer space. "What do you think?"

"Looks awesome," Kevin said, admiring her work.

TJ smiled and gave two enthusiastic thumbs-up,

while Warner rolled his eyes from across the shed and sat on a sack of nearly deflated soccer balls. He was flipping through the *Brainstorm* comic again. "Not that crazy about the name, but I like your logo, Tara."

"Thanks, crankface," Tara said, putting down her paints and brush.

"This thing looks nothing like the thing in my comic," Warner said, examining the illustrations.

"Stop being so negative," Kevin said. "We did everything it said to do, man. It's gonna work!"

"It better," said Tara as she wiped her paint-covered hands off on her clothes.

"It will," Kevin said, feeling pretty confident. "But we need to test it. Let's meet later tonight. Down by the lake. It's time to see what this thing can really do."

By quarter to eleven, a hush had fallen over the camp as the lights flicked out and everyone snuggled into bed. Well, everyone except for Kevin, Warner, TJ, and Tara, who were wide awake and getting ready for possibly their biggest night of camp ever.

Bailey had checked on the boys a little over an hour before and was now most likely listening to his headphones in bed, dozing.

Kevin threw off his covers and climbed off the top bunk, fully dressed and ready to go. Warner was on the bottom bunk, snoring loudly. TJ looked like he was asleep, too.

"Wake up, guys," said Kevin. "No time for snoozing."

"I'm just fake snoring," Warner said. "We all ready?"

TJ hopped off his bed, fully clothed, and opened the window.

Kevin grabbed his walkie-talkie, which was crackling with Tara's voice.

"Ten-four, fellas," Tara said softly. "Let's roll out. Over."

"Be right there," Kevin whispered. "Over."

Kevin, Warner, and TJ climbed out of their window and dropped to the ground, where Tara was waiting in the shadows. The four of them tiptoed down to the edge of the lake. The night sky was crystal clear, sparkling with hundreds of stars. It was the perfect night for a test transmission. They set up the galactascope where the shore rose up slightly and a row of tall reeds would hide them from view.

A chilly wind blew across the water. Kevin pulled the rip cord on the generator, and the motor rumbled into a smooth, steady hum. Tara flicked on the laser, which reflected off the pyrite's brassy metallic surface and refracted through the purple crystal.

"All right," Kevin said. "It's ready to go. . . ."

"Wait, you guys," said Tara. "We might be contacting aliens for maybe the first time ever. We could be making history right now! We need more than a hello."

"Okay, I got this," Warner said as he began to dictate their message to outer space. "Dear Aliens, What's up? We just want to say that we're totally peaceful, so if you want to meet up and exchange cultures, then we'd be down for that. As long as you, ya know, don't invade our minds or anything."

"Sounds good to me," said Kevin as TJ finished typing out the message.

Tara rolled her eyes and mumbled something to herself about boys.

The satellite dish tilted upward, aiming itself at the night sky. Kevin gave the thumbs-up and TJ hit the send button. Kevin felt his stomach clench as the laser refracted through the prism, shot out through the satellite dish, and carried their message to the universe across the black, starry night.

"So what happens now?" Kevin asked.

"We wait for the aliens," said Warner. "Obviously."

Kevin settled cross-legged into the grass and started to jot down the sequence of events in his log.

11:30 p.m.: No response yet.

11:37 p.m.: Tara challenges Warner and TJ to a staring contest. Warner blinks first. TJ wins.

11:38 p.m.: Warner challenges Tara to a laughing contest because that's what he thought they were doing in the first place. Tara laughs first.

11:45 p.m.: My butt is getting wet from the wet grass. Should have brought a towel.

11:50 p.m.: Everybody cranky. Warner regrets not bringing snacks. We all regret the no snack bringing, too.

12:00 a.m.: Galactascope still silent.

As Kevin marked the mission failure into his log, he felt his stomach tighten with panic. Even if there were aliens out there, it could take months for them to get the message, and they only had a few days before the convention.

"Come on, guys," Kevin said, his face crestfallen. "Let's pack up and get out of here before we get in trouble. We can try again tomorrow."

"Are you sure you don't want to wait a little longer, Kev?" Tara asked. "I could stay up a little laaaaaay-ter." She yawned, stretching her arms out.

THUNK! Tara's wrist whacked the device, and the galactascope abruptly began to blip and bleep. The laptop monitor flashed to life, and a long, repetitive jumble of ones and zeroes appeared on the screen.

"What'd you do?" Warner asked.

"I didn't mean to!" Tara scowled at Warner then looked at the computer. "What the heck is that?"

"It's a message," Kevin whispered, his voice tinged with anticipation.

They watched as the coded message scrolled down the computer screen, stopping abruptly and morphing into English through a neat little translator programming code that TJ had installed. "SOS. Need interstellar coordinates. SOS. Need interstellar coordinates. SOS."

"Quick," Warner said. "Send it a map of our solar system."

TJ typed frantically on the laptop, pulling up a diagram of Earth's solar system.

"Now give it our longitude and latitude," said Kevin.

They waited in suspense by the lakeside, hoping for a reply. "I don't know," Kevin said, beginning to get discouraged after ten minutes of silence. "Maybe someone's messing with us?"

"But no one knows we're even out here," Warner said.

Alexander, Kevin thought. *Is he spying on us?*

"Come on, Kevin," said Tara. "It has to be real. Let's try it again." She turned to TJ. "Resend the coordinates, Teej."

TJ nodded, interlocking his fingers and pushing out the palms of his hands. As his knuckles cracked, the night sky suddenly opened up with a bright neon-blue flash.

"Whoa," Warner and Tara said together.

Kevin blinked twice, completely speechless. He squinted and watched as a speck of otherworldly light started to grow against the dark backdrop of the sky. At first it looked like a normal star, but as the speck became larger and larger, Kevin could see a UFO hurtling toward them on a billowing trail of gray smoke. *This can't really be happening.*

"Get down!" Kevin shouted as the UFO flew right over their heads.

The four of them ducked for cover as the spacecraft crashed into the lake, sending a large wave rippling toward the shore.

"Holy Moley Mother of Cannoli!" TJ spoke for the first time since the beginning of camp. "Did you just see that?"

Tara, Warner, and Kevin all turned their heads to TJ.

"Dude," Warner said. "I totally forgot you even knew how to talk."

Kevin swiveled his head back and forth, waiting for one of their counselors to check out the commotion, but the camp was still.

"Omigosh," Tara cried out, pointing toward the center of the lake. Something had burst to the surface and was flailing frantically in the water.

"It can't swim," Kevin shouted, and ran toward the paddleboats that were beached on the lakeshore. "We gotta save it! Come on!"

At the lake's edge, Warner and Kevin dragged one of the boats into the water and hopped into the pedaling seats. Kevin's mind was reeling with the possibilities. They had actually summoned alien life to Earth, but if they didn't act quickly, it might all be for nothing!

"Hurry up, guys," Kevin called to Tara and TJ as they jumped into the back, rocking the boat unsteadily. A swell of water splashed over the side, soaking Kevin's sneakers and socks as he and Warner began to pedal fast toward the center of the lake.

As they drew closer to the drowning alien, Kevin watched the space creature gurgle one last breath and disappear below the surface, drifting down in a sinkhole of air bubbles.

Without thinking twice, Kevin tossed his glasses to Warner and jumped in after it. He dove straight down, blindly searching with his arms outstretched. After a few seconds, he grabbed hold of something that felt like the tail of a snake. Kevin gripped his hand around it and propelled himself back up to the surface, gasping for air, hoping with every particle in his body that this mystery creature was not about to bite his arm clean off.

Covered in fur, the smallish extraterrestrial weighed about as much as a bowling ball. It bobbed unconscious in the water as Kevin swam over to the paddleboat with their historic discovery tucked under one arm.

"TJ," Kevin gurgled into the lake water. "Gimme a hand." He used the rest of his strength to climb aboard while TJ and Warner hoisted the mammalian alien into the boat. Tara made a dirty-diaper face at the alien life form. "It's kind of smelly," she said from Kevin's seat as she started to pedal back.

"It's an alien," TJ's voice broke the silence. "What did you expect?"

As they reached the shore, Kevin and Warner jumped out and flopped the limp, wet blob of fur on its back in the grass. It was shaped like a toadstool with two skinny legs and a thick coat of dark purple fur. Beneath its wet pelt, the alien's body was leathery and translucent, and it had a set of four gangly arms.

"It looks dead." TJ poked the unconscious alien and flinched back with paranoid anticipation.

"This was so not a good idea," said Warner.

"I don't think it's breathing," Tara said, holding her palm above the creature's mouth. "And besides, the galactascope was *your* idea!"

"Actually, it was Max Greyson's idea. But what are we gonna do with a dead alien? Somebody needs to give it mouth-to-mouth." Warner tapped his nose and glared at Tara. "Not it."

"Not it," said Tara, touching her nose, too. "I'm not smooching that thing! What if I catch some weird alien virus? I'm not going out like that."

"I'll do it," Kevin said, ignoring his friends' game. He knelt down next to the sopping wet heap of extraterrestrial fur and stared at its face. Four different eyeballs stretched in a row across its head, all of them shut tight. Its fuzzy mouth sagged open, drooping in a small oval.

"Kev, don't," Warner said, placing his hand on his friend's shoulder. "What if she's right and you get, like, those squiggly little alien bacteria worms up your nose?"

"Don't worry, little guy. We're gonna save you," Kevin said, ignoring Warner. He took a deep breath and lowered his head face-to-face with the unconscious extraterrestrial. On his way down, he caught a whiff of the alien's musky odor—a mix of raw chicken juice and an unbathed sheepdog— and choked back a gag.

"Gross!" Kevin gasped, and then pinched his nose to take another breath. As he leaned over the alien a second time, it jerked to life, coughing a spurt of slimy lake water right into Kevin's face.

"Ugh!" Kevin jumped back from the critter and wiped the spit off his nose with the sleeve of his sweatshirt. "Why'd you let me do that?" he asked his friends while spitting out more alien mucus.

"We told you not to," Tara and Warner said together, and shrugged.

"Urrgh . . . yuck!" Kevin kept finding more alien upchuck on his neck and earlobes.

"Uh, guys," TJ said, his eyes bulging.

Kevin, Warner, and Tara turned their attention back to the alien, whose quartet of eyeballs had just fluttered open. It sat up and scanned their faces.

"Are you the ones?" it asked.

"The ones?" Tara asked, furrowing her brow.

"Are you the ones who called?" it spoke again.

"Yes," said Kevin, now moving toward the extraterrestrial fur ball. "My name is Kevin Brewer. And these are my friends Warner, Tara, and TJ."

"Uh-huh-huh," the three of them stuttered over one another, dumbfounded.

The alien moved to get up. Upright, it stood about three feet tall, coming up to Kevin's hip. Jutting out from its drenched purple pelt, the space creature's boneless, hairless arms moved fluidly like gigantic spaghetti noodles.

"I am Mim," the alien said as he took in his surroundings. "This is Earth?"

"That's right." Tara stepped forward, now between Warner and Kevin. "Welcome to our home." She raised her arm slowly to shake Mim's three-fingered hand.

"Don't leave her hanging, man," Warner said to Mim, and mimicked a handshake.

Mim narrowed his eyes, not understanding, and then his entire body shook involuntarily, like a dog after a swim. Kevin backed up and clenched his eyes closed as drops of smelly lake water sprayed across his face. When Mim was finished, his fur puffed out like an angry cat's tail.

Tara started to giggle. "He's actually sort of cute!"

"Wow, Mim, it's a real honor to meet you!" TJ stepped forward in front of the alien, looking absolutely fascinated. "Have you been to Earth before? What's your favorite color? What do you eat on your planet? What type of alien are you? That is, if there's more than one type . . . What do your parents do? Do aliens even have parents? Mine are both doctors. . . ." TJ went on and on, asking every possible question that popped into his head, but Mim just stared at him blankly. "Oh man, I have so many questions. . . . What type of warp drive engine does your spaceship have? I mean, you must have some kind of warp drive if you're traveling through the galaxy so quickly. Unless you're using wormholes. Are you using wormholes? Or maybe you're utilizing both. . . ."

Mim looked at Kevin and then back at TJ. Kevin just shrugged. The fuzzy alien seemed like he might keel over at any second, like a punch-drunk boxer at the end of a fight.

"TJ, give him a break," Kevin said, then turned to Mim. "Sorry, he doesn't usually talk this much."

"Yeah," said Warner. "He doesn't normally talk at all."

"Why don't we find you a place to stay and rest?" Kevin said.

Mim nodded, and his eyes blinked rapidly. "Yes."

"Great! Then it's settled. You'll bunk with us!" Kevin said with an ear-to-ear grin on his face.

"Uh, buddy?" Warner said to Kevin. "Can we talk for a quick sec?"

Kevin raised his index finger at Mim and stepped away to huddle up with his team. "What's up?"

"Okay, first of all, I want to point out that that's a real live alien over there and it's talking to us," Warner said. "Just putting that out there."

"I know," Tara said, her eyes wide with wonder.

"But he can't stay in our cabin." Warner stood back and crossed his arms.

"Sure he can," said Kevin. "He can sleep under the bed."

"Dude, you're not thinking straight," Warner said. "What if someone finds him?"

"Yeah," TJ chimed in. "Someone who'd want to hurt him or take him away from us."

"No way we're going to let that happen," said Kevin. "This is our alien!" He pulled off his hoodie and handed the sweatshirt to Mim. "Here, put this on in case any-one's spying. We can take you to the sports shed instead."

Mim put on the hoodie and followed the group back through camp, sneaking behind the mess hall. A light was still on in the cabin where the counselors on night duty were stationed. Kevin tiptoed behind the cabin and saw junior counselors Cody and Nick playing Guitar Hero on the TV inside the lounge. They were both wear-ing large headphones, rocking out on some heavy metal song.

"We're in the clear, guys," Kevin said. "Let's go."

When they arrived at the shed, the padlock on the door glimmered faintly in the lunar light.

"Shoot," said Kevin. "I forgot they keep this thing locked after hours."

"Don't worry, I know the combo. I had to get some badminton rackets out of here once for Bailey," said Tara as she approached the door. "Three-fourteen-fifteen. The first five digits of pi."

Spin-spin-clink! Tara unhooked the lock and the door swung open.

Mim walked in first, his stride somewhere between a waddle and a strut.

A swath of spiderwebs hung overhead. Kevin shuddered at the thought of one of those plump, juicy spiders dropping down in front of his face.

"We can try to set you up somewhere better tomorrow, but this is the best place for tonight," Kevin said.

"Hmmm," Mim hummed, gazing around at the spider-infested shed cluttered with ancient sports equipment. "Perfect!" His eyes sparkled gratefully. "How can I thank you?"

"For starters," Warner said, "you can promise to stay here. And don't let anyone else besides us see you."

"Yeah," said Tara. "We'll pick you up tomorrow after second lab."

"That I can do," Mim said. "Sleep tight, Earthlings. Don't let the klink-klops bite."

"Hah! Okay, Mim. G'night!" Kevin said, as he clicked the padlock back into place. *What the heck are klink-klops?* Kevin thought, when two bright beams of light swooped through the darkness.

"It's Nick and Cody," Warner whispered, and motioned for everyone to freeze in place. Kevin's heart began to race, *thumpity-thump thump.*

"We gotta make a break for it," Tara said. "They're headed this way."

Kevin nodded for everyone to go ahead. Tara took off in a tiptoed sprint back to her bunk, and Warner and TJ trailed behind. Kevin watched as the three of them ducked into the shadows and then he took off, too, dodging the watchmen's waggling flashlights.

When Kevin reached the side of his cabin, Warner and TJ were there waiting. Kevin dug his hands into the surrounding bushes and pulled out a small stepladder that he had hidden so they could boost themselves through the open window. But before the boys could climb inside, Cody rounded the back of the bunkhouse and caught Kevin's sleeve in the glare of his bright light.

Kevin, Warner, and TJ pressed their backs against the cabin. The three of them hushed up and shuffled back into the shadows. *We're so busted!* Kevin thought.

Then TJ opened his mouth, and with a shift of his jaw and a twist of his lips, he cried out. "Help! Help!" The strange voice sounded like it was coming from far off.

Cody spun around, away from the boys, and trained his flashlight on the bushes. "Uh-oh," he said. "Someone's in trouble."

"You hear that?" Nick said, panting as he ran up behind.

"Yeah," said Cody. "It sounded like it was coming from over there." He pointed to the edge of the woods.

Kevin let out a deep breath as the two counselors dashed off into the forest.

"Yo, man," said Kevin to TJ. "That was awesome. How'd you make your voice sound like it was all the way over there?"

"Oh, I was a ventriloquist for a couple years," he said with shrug. "I got pretty good at it."

"I'll say." Warner made a fist and held it up to TJ for a pound. "Glad your vocal cords are working again, my man."

Kevin stepped on the ladder and headed into their bedroom. "Let's get inside before Nick and Cody get back."

After putting on pajamas and getting ready for bed, Kevin pulled out the logbook to enter one more note.

23 June 2014, 12:15–12:45 a.m.: Hung out with a real live alien!

Lying on his back on the top bunk, Kevin was still wide awake. Warner wasn't catching many winks down below either. Across the room on the single bed, TJ was so revved up with energy that he was already composing another list of questions for Mim, which he said in a whisper as he wrote.

"What are other aliens like? Are we all in the same universe or are there parallel universes? What star system supports your home planet?"

"Come on, Teej," Kevin said. "We're all glad you're talking again, but we need to get some rest."

"Really, Kev?" Warner said. "How do you expect us

to sleep right now? We just proved that alien life exists. We're gonna be, like, super famous."

"Yeah, Kevin," said TJ. "I think we pretty much have the Invention Convention in the bag."

"Yeah, we didn't just catch a glimpse of him either," Kevin said, getting into it. "We saved his life!"

"He's our boy now, dude," Warner said.

"Wait," said TJ. "How do we even know he's a boy? Maybe Mim's not a him at all. I mean, his entire species could be one gender. I have to write this down. . . ."

"Did you see that spaceship he had, too?" Warner asked. "That thing was sick!"

"Yeah," Kevin said. "Way sweeter than the VMN's hovercraft!" He rolled on his side and looked out the window. "Now we just need to make sure no one finds Mim before the conven—"

"What the—?" Kevin hopped off the top bunk and pressed his face to the glass as a sudden flash of light lit up the windowpane. Warner and TJ followed, looking over his shoulders.

Outside the bunk, a two-legged figure that looked

like a giant praying mantis appeared as if zapped in from another dimension. It stood well over six feet tall and wore a shiny cybertronic space suit, like something straight out of a sci-fi movie. A really awesome sci-fi movie. The fact that it was making a beeline for the sports shed, though, was not so awesome.

"Mim!" Kevin said.

"Come on," said TJ, lifting up the window.

"No way I'm going out there," Warner said. "Did you see that thing?"

"Don't be a fraidy cat," said TJ, slipping one leg over the windowsill.

"Shhhh!" Kevin ordered them both to be quiet.

As the boys snuck out of their cabin, a faint noise caught their attention from near the mess hall. "Psst!" Tara peered around the building and summoned the boys over. She was quivering and could barely form a word. "Big bug . . . ," she muttered.

"Two aliens in one night! And one of them's a cyborg insectoid!" TJ whispered, barely able to contain his excitement. He pinched himself. "Okay, good . . . ," he said, then reached over and pinched Kevin's arm.

"Ouch, man!" Kevin grabbed his shoulder.

"Sorry, I had to make sure I wasn't dreaming," said TJ.

"What does that have to do with pinching me?"

"Because I had to make sure I wasn't in your dream either."

Kevin shook his head as they edged back around

the sports shed. The door was slightly ajar, and something metallic glistened on the ground. Kevin crawled ahead of the group and crouched down, then picked up the metal object in the grass. He swallowed a painful cry as his skin touched the metal and then immediately dropped the piece back on the ground. "It burned me!" he whispered under his breath, clutching his seared skin. "Ouch!"

Warner crept up next to Kevin and kicked the object in the grass. "It's the padlock," he said. "It looks like it's been cut clean in half with a laser."

TJ was already at the partly opened door, squinting through his thick prescription glasses into the dark shed. He looked back at Kevin, Warner, and Tara. "It's in there," he whispered.

Kevin was

almost too scared to go in. The only thing making him move closer was his own curiosity. He tiptoed forward and peered through the doorway. The extraterrestrial insectoid's back was to them, and it towered silently over Mim's slumbering form. Then it pulled out a small handheld device from its cybertronic suit and aimed the scope right at Mim's furry belly.

Kevin's stomach plummeted to his knees. "Hey!" he barked loudly, and flung open the door. "Get away from him!"

The insectoid spun away from Mim and trained its gaze on the doorway. It opened its mouth and uttered a strange guttural clacking noise in its alien tongue.

TJ jumped forward, stepping up before the beast. "Maybe you're hard of hearing, but he said get away from our alien."

The mantis let out another hideous, bleating yowl that had it not been for the glass helmet around its praying mantis head would have woken the entire camp.

TJ flinched and jumped behind Warner.

The gigantic insectoid lifted its arms and scoped

the kids in the crosshairs of its weapon.

"Duck!" Kevin yelled as a bright magenta laser beam shot out from the high-tech contraption. ZAMMO! The laser struck a barrel filled with badminton rackets and seared a hole through the middle of the bin.

"Coooooool," said TJ. "A real photon blaster!"

In the commotion, Mim blinked his eyes awake and then pounced on the mantis's arm.

"Gluck-gluck-Mim-yim-yarkle," the mantis growled, fending off the purple alien, and shot another laser beam in Kevin's direction.

PYOO-HOO! The laser beam squealed and zapped a large bag of soccer balls, which flashed brightly and disappeared.

Mim let out a growl like an angry house cat and leaped into the air. He grabbed ahold of the bug's glass helmet with two of his arms and pulled, leveraging his feet on the alien's shoulders.

The praying mantis backed up, trying to pry Mim off its head. But Mim held on tight and unleashed a four-hit combo that shattered the insectoid's protective helmet to pieces.

The alien mantis fell to the floor of the shed with a clatter, now unconscious after breathing in Earth's poisonous air.

Mim jumped off the giant bug and pried the insectoid's photon blaster out of its claws. With the flip of a switch, he activated the machine's de-atomizer and flashed a beam at the fallen predator. Kevin, Warner, Tara, and TJ stood stock-still as the insectoid alien vanished into thin air. They were safe, but Kevin could barely believe what he'd just seen.

"Wh-what the heck was that thing and why was it trying to kill you?" Tara interrupted.

"And us!" added Warner.

Mim thought for a moment. "It's kind of a long story—that was Zeff. He's been after me for as long as I can remember." Mim sat down on a basket of tennis balls and took a deep breath. "This isn't easy for me to talk about, but I will tell you." He ran his hands through his fuzzy purple pelt. "You see this?" he said, tugging on a tuft. "For two millennia space poachers from all over the galaxy have been after my species, hunting us down and killing us for our fur so they can make coats out of us. It can get really cold in outer space." Mim hopped down from the basket.

"I've been on the run for almost a decade, hiding out, trying not to get caught. And thanks to the signal you sent out, I was finally able to warp through space-time and reach Earth, a place to call home if you'll have me."

Tara's eyes brimmed with tears, and TJ was speechless once again. Warner's face was fixed in an expression of disbelief. Kevin gulped down the knot that was beginning to form in the back of his throat. Mim was in trouble, and they had to help him.

"Are there going to be more of those things coming after you?" Warner said finally.

Mim nodded. "Most likely. Hopefully not right away. It's pretty difficult to trace the wormhole network. Almost impossible to keep track of who goes where."

"So you do use wormholes," TJ said. "I knew it!"

Mim's attention turned to a big fat spider scuttling across the floor. Kevin watched as Mim reached down and grabbed the eight-legged bug by one leg, letting it dangle in front of his four-eyed face.

"Oops, I must have missed this one earlier." The furry little alien popped the spider into his mouth and chewed furiously.

"Ew, you just ate that spider!" Tara proclaimed. "Gross!"

Kevin looked up at the ceiling. All the spiderwebs and spiders from earlier were now gone.

Mim belched. "I was starving!"

"Dude, we can bring you some real snacks tomorrow," said Warner. "I'll even give you the team discount."

"Really?" Mim said, licking a spider leg that was stuck to his finger. "I can be part of the team?"

"Of course," said Kevin with a smile. "Listen, we should probably get back to our bunks. Are you sure you're going to be all right in here for the night?"

"I think so. I'll sleep with one eye open just in case." Mim closed three of his eyes and winked with the other one.

"G'night, Mim," Kevin bid their new alien friend farewell for the second time that night and closed the door.

The next day, Kevin could barely stay awake during his afternoon astronomy lab. It didn't help that they were in the dark planetarium either.

The guest lecturer had canceled and Camp Director Dimpus was the substitute, fumbling through a PowerPoint on the gravitational fields of supermassive black holes. It was the perfect time to take a little nap. Kevin already knew all there was to know about black holes anyway. His eyes grew heavy as he slumped in his seat, listening to the drone of Dimpus's lecture.

A few moments later, Kevin felt an elbow jam into his ribs. "Stop snoring, dude," Warner said. "You're gonna get us in trouble."

Two rows ahead, Alexander turned around and shot them a sourpuss. "Some of us are trying to pay attention."

Kevin opened his eyes and sat up straighter. The clock on the wall read quarter to four, only fifteen more minutes till they could go see Mim again. When the minute hand finally reached the twelve and the lesson came to an end, Kevin, Warner, and TJ bolted out the door and back to their cabin. TJ grabbed a pencil and started adding a few more questions to his list of things to ask Mim. Warner gathered up a bunch of candy bars, and Kevin grabbed an empty duffel bag from under his bed in case they needed to transport Mim. They had to be extra careful not to let him be seen by anyone, especially with Alexander watching them closely.

The walkie-talkie on the desk crackled, and Tara's voice radioed in. "Hey, boys, heading over to see you know who. See you in a few! Over."

"We'll be there in five," Kevin said.

"Come on," TJ said, racing out the door. "Last one

there's a purple alien!"

When they reached the sports shed, Tara was already inside, but Mim was nowhere to be found. A knot of worry began to form in Kevin's belly.

"Wait," Warner said. "You don't think more insectoids found him?"

Kevin, Warner, Tara, and TJ searched around the shed frantically, pushing aside bins filled with orange and blue pinnies and digging through piles of baseball mitts. Kevin was about to look through the tennis equipment when he heard a rustle come from behind them.

"What are you nerdbombers doing in the sports shed?" Alexander said as the Vainglorious Math Nerds came up from behind them.

"Actually," said Tara, "we're having a supersecret meeting and you're not welcome."

"Oh really?" Alexander said. "How is the new project coming along? Spying on anyone else today? I hear Team Quasar's working on a soda pop that makes your hair turn a different color."

"None of your beeswax," said Kevin.

"Actually, it would be my beeswax," Alexander retorted. "I'm president of the Beekeepers Club."

Warner glared at Alexander. "I don't think it qualifies as a club if there's only one member."

"We're members, too," said Dante and Luke.

"And you each have one third of a brain, give or take," said TJ. "So that still only makes one member. Sorry, guys."

"Oh, so it really does talk," Alexander said, patting TJ on the noggin. TJ flinched and glowered at the bully. "I was starting to worry. There was a rumor going around that you'd been abducted by aliens."

"Yeah, right," said Kevin nervously. "Like aliens actually exist."

"You don't believe in aliens?" Alexander scoffed, turning to Luke and Dante. "He doesn't believe in aliens! What a lamebrain!"

"Whatever, Alexander," Kevin said. "We'll see what happens at the convention."

"Whatever is right, Brewer. You've got no chance." Before he stalked off with his minions in tow, Alexander stooped to the floor just inside the door and picked something up from the ground. He held it up curiously, pinching a little tuft of purple fur between his thumb and forefinger.

"Hmmm," Alexander said. "I've never seen anything like this!"

"I don't know," Warner said. "Maybe it's from one of Team Quasar's soda experiments?"

Alexander glowered at Warner. "Maybe, but that means their soda works! We better get this back to the lab, boys."

Kevin's stomach dropped. They couldn't let Alexander make off with a sample of their alien, but Tara was all over it.

"Watch out," Tara yelled as she smacked the tuft of fur free from Alexander's grip. The fur went flying in every direction like the puffs of a dandelion.

"Hey!" Alexander growled at her. "That was my specimen!"

"Sorry," she said. "There was, like, a super-huge mosquito about to nibble your arm."

Alexander's eyes narrowed, and his lips curled up into a sneer.

"Who cares, Alexander?" Luke said to his captain. "Let's get out of here."

"Yeah, you're right," Alexander said, staring at Kevin. "Time to leave these losers to their losing."

"See ya," said Tara as the VMNs walked off. "Wouldn't want to be ya."

Once Alexander and his cronies were gone, Kevin went back to searching for their extraterrestrial friend.

"Mim!" Kevin called out in a whisper. "Mim!"

They all heard a crash that sounded like it was coming from outside the shed, and Kevin braced himself for another Alexander intrusion.

"Hello, friends," Mim said as he darkened the doorway to the shed. He waved with one hand while holding a couple of wet suits and a scuba tank in his three other hands.

Kevin breathed a deep sigh of relief. "Where've you been, Mim? We thought you got kidnapped . . . or alien-napped or whatever."

"It'll take more than a de-atomizer to take me out, trust me," Mim said. "Do any of you have something to eat? I ran out of spiders."

"No problem, Mim," Warner said. "I got just the thing." He tossed the fluffy little alien two candy bars and a couple of bags of chips. Mim dropped his gear and caught each snack item with a different hand. "Try these. Way better than spiders."

Mim's mouth widened to twice its normal size, and he tossed all four in at once, wrappers and all. "Mmm . . ."

"No, dude, you're not supposed to—" Warner started to say. "Never mind."

"So, Mim," TJ said, producing the neatly folded-up list of questions. "I have a few more things I want to ask you."

"Shoot," said Mim, wriggling his tongue to dislodge

a piece of candy wrapper stuck in his teeth. The bit of plastic wrapper seemed to dissolve as he salivated. "I'm feeling much livelier today."

"Do all aliens know how to speak English?"

"No, only those of us who have a language chip."

Mim pulled back a thatch of fur on the side of his head to reveal something square and bulging from under the skin. "It's a computer chip that translates for your brain. I don't even have to think about it."

"Sweet," said Warner, sounding a little bummed. "We still have to learn stuff the old-fashioned way."

"Speaking of old-fashioned, who here knows how to use these things?" Mim said, picking up the scuba gear again.

"I do," said Kevin. "And so does Warner."

"We took scuba last summer," said Warner. "We even got the gold medal at the scuba scavenger hunt."

"Do you think you could use your gold medal skills and get my stuff from the lake? If we don't get my supplies, we're not going to stand a chance against any other poachers."

"I guess we could do it," said Kevin. "We've never dived down that far, though." He chewed a fingernail.

"But you'll do it?" Mim asked, and the four Extraordinary Terrestrials nodded. "Great! You guys are the best. Tonight, we dive."

After sundown, Kevin and Warner were back in their room, pulling on their wet suits. A tuft of bright orange hair flopped out of Kevin's black scuba cap, and he tucked it back under, trying to smooth out the rubber. He turned to TJ, who was awkwardly trying to wear his glasses underneath the goggles. Kevin had borrowed a spare pair of Warner's contact lenses, and since they had the exact same prescription, Kevin could see fine.

"I guess I couldn't go anyway," TJ said, giving up and fumbling to put his eyeglasses back in place.

"Don't worry, dude," Kevin said. "You and Tara both have important jobs."

"Yeah, man," said Warner. "You're our eyes and ears. If anything's about to go down, just give us the heads-up."

TJ held up the walkie-talkie and saluted them both. "You know I got your back."

Warner went back to checking himself out in the mirror. "I look pretty good in this thing, huh?"

"Yeah, if by good, you mean—"

Knock-knock!

"Who's there?" Kevin asked as his perfectly worded wet-suit insult slipped his mind.

"Check-in time," Bailey said on the other side of the door.

"Check-in time who?" Warner said, taking the goggles away from TJ and stuffing them under his pillow.

"Come on, little dudes. I haven't got all night." Bailey's voice grew irritable behind the door.

Kevin yanked off the swimming cap and he and Warner quickly threw on pajama pants and sweatshirts over the wet suits.

"One second!" Warner said, pushing the rest of the diving equipment under the bed. "I'm just getting dressed."

Kevin opened the door, now wearing his pajama

bottoms. "Hey, Bailey." His counselor towered over him.

"Hi, fellas," Bailey said. "What are you guys up to?"

"Up to?" said Kevin, trying to sound carefree. "Whole lot of nothin'."

"Is that true, Warner?" their counselor asked.

"Yeah, I mean nothing's going on," Warner said. "Why?"

"We're supposed to be on the lookout," said Bailey. "Apparently, there've been some reports of certain strange goings-on around here lately."

"Goings-on?" asked Kevin, playing stupid.

"You know," Bailey said. "Campers sneaking out at night. Flashing lights. You guys don't know anything about that, do you?"

"Nope," said Warner, his eyes darting away to the scuba flipper sticking out from under the bed.

"Good," Bailey said, scribbling something on his clipboard. Then he chuckled to himself. "One camper even claims he saw a monster prowling around the campgrounds. You kids have the craziest imaginations."

"You know us kids," Kevin said, laughing nervously, when suddenly there was a rapping underneath Warner's window.

"Are you guys expecting company?" Bailey asked.

Kevin jumped to the windowsill and peered out. Mim was standing on the ground below. "There's nobody there."

"Must have been a squirrel or something," said TJ.

"Yo, you're talking!" their counselor said. "I just won twenty bucks off Cody. Ha ha! I knew you could talk."

TJ shrugged and looked away nonchalantly.

"All right, sleep well, fellas," Bailey said as he headed to the common room. "See you tomorrow."

As the door to the bedroom closed, Kevin sighed loudly and started pulling out the scuba gear from under the bed. Warner and TJ ran to the window, where Mim was waiting.

Warner climbed over TJ's bed and lifted the window. Mim hopped up nimbly, bounding over the sill onto the mattress, then bounced onto the floor. "Howdy, partners! You guys ready?"

"Soon," Warner said, as they finished putting on their diving gear.

"Dude, that was way too close!" Kevin said. "We've got to start being more careful."

At the edge of the lakeshore Kevin and Warner put on their flippers, secured their goggles, and checked the oxygen tanks. Kevin looked down at his waterproof watch and pressed the glow button so he could see in the dark.

"Okay," he whispered. "The night patrol should have passed by the lake already. We should be good to go."

"Come in, Tango-Alpha-Romeo. Tango-Juliet. Over," Warner said into his walkie-talkie. They'd come up with new code names for one another earlier that day. "Remember, you guys are the lookouts. If you see anybody heading our way, call Mim on this radio."

"Got it." TJ's voice crackled through the transmitter a bit loudly.

"Be careful, you guys," Tara chimed in.

"We will." Kevin turned the volume down a little lower.

"So, what's the plan, Mim? Where is this stuff?" Warner asked, handing him the walkie-talkie for safekeeping.

"For you and you." Mim handed each of them a folded piece of paper.

Kevin opened up the note to reveal a hand-drawn map of the alien spacecraft. "Whoa." The craft was shaped like a flattened diamond, with two long wings stretching out on either side. There was a point at the top and another at the bottom, where a small exit hatch had been marked with an arrow.

"The exit shaft will still be open," Mim said, motioning to the small square door on the map. "Get the black bag underneath the seat in the cockpit. That's the stuff we need."

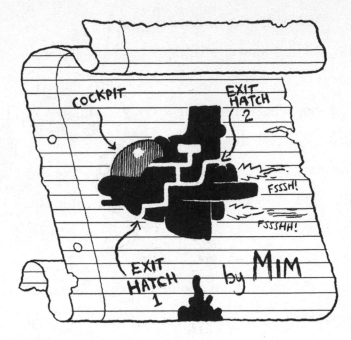

Kevin and Warner studied the diagram closely, committing the map to memory. A circular corridor ran around the interior of the ship, and the cockpit was positioned at the front, opposite the exit shaft. "Got it," Kevin said, and handed his paper back to Mim.

"You ready?" Warner asked Kevin. The boys faced the middle of the lake, where Mim's spaceship had plunged just the other night. Kevin and Warner lowered their goggles and double-checked their air tanks.

"Let's do this," Kevin responded.

The boys put in their mouthpieces and waded into the shallow water. When it got deep enough, Kevin dove, wriggling his legs and kicking his flippers, propelling himself to the bottom of the lake. Now below the surface, the boys flicked on their underwater flashlights and immediately saw the sunken spaceship wedged in the sand like a Frisbee that had landed cockeyed.

As they approached, the beams of light wavered through the dark volume of water and shined down on the open hatch of Mim's submerged ship.

The two boys swam through the door and turned down a narrow steel corridor until they reached the cockpit. High-tech control panels lined the large window in front of a fancy pilot seat, and some kind of transparent helmet hung above it.

Kevin kicked his flippers together like a dolphin and zipped through the underwater spacecraft to the base of the pilot seat. He reached underneath, feeling for a strap handle. When his hand grazed the bag Mim had described, he pulled on it hard. With a pop and a flurry of bubbles, the bag burst out from under the seat and swayed in the water while Kevin held on tight.

He glanced over to give Warner the thumbs-up, but his friend was distracted, training the light on something behind Kevin. Warner pointed, his eyes wide with fear. As Kevin saw what Warner was looking at, his heart skipped a beat. A mutant octopus monster twice the size of an adult lion swam in place. It stared at them with the face of a tarantula.

Kevin turned back to Warner, whose eyes were still popping out of their sockets. They had to get out of there. But when Kevin moved an inch, the alien beast

stirred, revealing a set of four thick arachnid-like legs covered in coarse hair.

The creature extended one of its five-foot-long tentacles toward them, and Warner shrieked. A torrent of air bubbles shot out of his scuba mouthpiece as Kevin grabbed Warner's arm and swam away through the spacecraft's circular passageway. Looking over his shoulder, Kevin saw a dark blur of movement whoosh past his line of vision as the spider-fish rounded the corner fast.

The boys shot out of the exit hatch and kicked their flippers, swimming for their lives toward the surface. As they burst out of the water, Kevin could see Mim waving them in to shore excitedly, but they weren't out of harm's way yet. Behind them, the water stirred and rippled and the head of the alien octo-spider rose from the depths of the lake. The alien lake monster bobbed like a lurking crocodile and then disappeared back underneath.

"Whoa," Kevin mumbled through his mouthpiece, holding on tightly to Mim's black bag as the boys swam frantically toward the shore.

"Come on, Kevin!" Warner shouted from ahead. "Don't look back!"

Kevin caught up with Warner, and they both raced out of the lake onto dry land. Kevin dropped the bag on the ground with a *clank*, then took out his mouthpiece. "What the heck," he gasped, "was that thing, Mim?"

"My apologies," said Mim. "I should have warned you guys about Poobah."

"Poobah?" Kevin repeated, taking a puff of his inhaler, which he had left ashore.

"That thing almost made me poobah in my pants," Warner said.

Mim shrugged. "He's harmless, unless you make him mad."

"So what is he?" Kevin asked.

"He's an arachnopod," Mim told them.

"So he's part spider," Warner said. "But you eat spiders."

"I couldn't eat an arachnopod if I wanted to," Mim said. "Poobah belongs to one of the few species that are completely inedible because of the poison ink running through them."

"Aren't you scared he'll eat you?" Kevin asked. "He's way bigger than you are."

"He can't," said Mim. "He's very allergic to my fur. Quite vexing. He sneezes all over the place, but he makes a great guard pet."

Mim stared down at his bag and rubbed his hands together as if he were about to dig into a delicious meal. He opened the bag, revealing a small stockpile of sleek alien gadgets and gizmos dazzling in the moonlight.

"Code red, code red," TJ's voice crackled faintly over the walkie-talkie's receiver. "I just saw someone sneak out of one of the other bunks. I didn't get a clear look. It might just be a sleepwalker."

"I got a visual," Tara said. "The subject is headed your way. I repeat, the subject is headed your way."

Kevin and Warner both whirled around, looking for any sign of someone coming. "Who is it?" Kevin asked.

"Not positive, but I think it's you know who—"

"Hey!" a voice rang out from behind them.

Kevin and Warner spun around while Mim jumped into the bag and zipped it half shut.

Alexander Russ walked out of the woods and made his way toward the shore. "You little phlegmwads are out way past curfew. Naughty, naughty."

"What, are you gonna rat us out?" Warner said. "You're not back in your bunk either. You tell on us, you get in trouble too."

"Do you know how much money my dad's company donates to this camp? They couldn't kick me out if they tried." Alexander took a step toward the bag at Kevin's feet when—*ZAP!* A bright white-and-blue pulse of light lit up the trees. Kevin was blinded by the flash, and when his eyes focused again, Alexander was standing stiff as a board, his face stuck in an expression of hateful delight.

"Whoa!" Warner exclaimed, gawking at the frozen nerd bully.

Kevin turned and saw Mim holding one of the gadgets from his bag. The device was reflective and looked like a circular iPad. A series of colored buttons ran along the back, and two grooved handles curved out on either side. The grips were fashioned with what could have been the handbrakes on a bicycle.

"He's just frozen." Mim lowered the freeze ray. "I had to do something. He was going to turn you in. Pretty cool, huh?"

Kevin walked up to Alexander and waved his hand back and forth in front of his face. "Is he gonna be okay?"

"Don't worry, he'll be fine. The freeze ray doesn't actually freeze him, just hits him with an electromagnetic pulse to put him in a state of suspended animation," Mim said. "He'll wake up in a couple hours thinking he dreamt this whole thing."

"We gotta get him back to his bunk," Warner said.

"Yeah, and quick," said Kevin. "Cody and Nick are on night duty again tonight."

"I'll get his arms," said Warner. "You get his feet."

"Go on. I got the bag." Mim slung the black bag of alien gadgets over his shoulder. "I'll keep watch while you go put this guy to bed."

As they lugged their freeze-rayed nemesis back to his bunk, the light flicked on in the counselor's room. Kevin and Warner ducked quickly into the shadows, flattening their backs against the wall directly below the window.

Above them, the counselor stuck his head outside his

window and yawned. In the distance, a wild dog howled, and the counselor shut the window to return to bed.

The boys tiptoed up the steps, edged inside the bunkhouse, and walked softly down to the last room in the hallway. They backed into the door to Alexander's room. The door opened with a creak. "Shhhh," Warner shushed as they paused on the threshold. Alexander's roommates, Dante and Luke, were both sleeping soundly. Dante wore a heavy nighttime orthodontic headset and snored rather loudly. A puddle of drool spilled from Luke's sleeping mouth onto his Batman pillowcase.

Warner and Kevin lugged Alexander across the dark room, moving slowly, carefully trying to hush every footstep. Halfway across the room, Luke shifted in his bed with a grunt, and Warner and Kevin paused. After a long, breathless silence, Luke rolled back over, still in a deep snooze.

"Come on," Warner whispered as they reached Alexander's bedside. "Set him down. Nice and easy."

Kevin sighed with relief as he and Warner swung

Alexander gently onto his bottom bunk. Kevin awkwardly tucked him in and pulled the covers up to hide his frozen face.

"Alexander?" said a sleepy voice across the room. Dante had woken up. "That you?"

Kevin looked at Warner, who was crouching at the foot of Alexander's bed. He pressed his index finger to his lips and then ducked down flat on the floor.

"Alexander . . . ," Dante's voice whispered again.

"Yuh-huh?" Kevin cupped his hand over his mouth and did his best Alexander impression while slowly crawling toward the door.

"You awake?"

Kevin and Warner rushed out the still-open door before they blew their cover and hightailed it back to their bunk as fast as their legs could carry them. They snuck past the lab trailers and tiptoed to their own window. Already standing behind the glass, TJ lifted it up and sent down the rope ladder.

"What took you guys so long?" TJ asked as they climbed back inside. "I thought you got caught for sure!"

"Umm, we kind of just freeze-rayed Alexander," Kevin said.

TJ's eyes twinkled as he furrowed his brow, confused but clearly liking the idea. "Where's Mim?"

In a flash, Mim appeared on the window ledge, the bag of gear slung over his shoulder.

"Are you sure he's going to be okay?" Warner asked Mim.

"Don't worry about a thing. He's going to be fine," Mim said. "Do you guys want to hang out? I can tell you more about how the freeze ray works."

"I would but I'm pretty pooped," said Kevin.

Warner yawned. "Me too. That arachnopod kind of wore me out."

"What's an arachnopod?" TJ asked, his ears perking up.

"We'll fill you in later," said Kevin.

"Hey, Mim?" Warner said, going to his suitcase, where he kept his candy stash. "You want some snacks for the road?"

Mim made a "yummy" noise and his mouth nearly stretched the entire width of his face. "Oh, yes, please."

Warner passed a few candy bars and some chips to Kevin, who handed them to Mim. "No need to eat the wrappers this time, buddy, okay?"

Mim looked at them all funny. "But that's the best part."

He cracked a smile, and TJ busted out in loud laughter.

"Wait," Kevin said as Mim was about to hop out the window. "Take this, too." He handed their fuzzy little friend their spare walkie-talkie. "So you can call us."

Perched on the windowsill, Mim looked down at his new Earthling friends. "Good job tonight, boys. Tomorrow we're going to have some real fun."

The next day after lunch the boys were hanging out in their cabin during free time. After another late night, the three of them were dozing off when they heard banging on their door.

"Open up. It's time for your spot check," Cody's voice boomed through the door.

Kevin opened the door, and Cody and Nick pushed their way inside. "We got a tip some campers have been selling candy out of their bunks. That's a big no-no."

Kevin lowered his gaze, trying to avoid eye contact with Warner. They could get disqualified from the Invention Convention if the counselors found Warner's secret stash. Cody and Nick began to search the room, looking under beds and in drawers.

"Aw, come on, fellas," TJ said as they pulled back the sheets on the beds and checked under the mattresses. "I just remade that, like, five minutes ago."

Just as they were about to move on to the next room Cody went to the closet where Warner kept his stash in one of his suitcases. A bead of sweat ran down Kevin's forehead.

Cody bent down and unzipped the luggage.

Warner winced with one eye open as Cody looked up from the open suitcase and stared at the boys.

"Nothing," he said, looking to Nick.

"No candy stash?" Nick asked, sounding slightly disappointed.

"I guess you're off the hook," Cody said. "If you see anyone with candy around here, be sure to let us know."

"Will do, officers," TJ said, and did a quick salute.

As soon as Nick and Cody were out the door, Kevin breathed out a sigh of relief. Warner raced over to the suitcase and looked inside. He gasped. "What the—?"

Kevin went over to see for himself, and TJ followed close behind.

Except for a few random tufts of Mim's purple fur, the suitcase was completely empty. Warner's entire stash of candy was gone.

"Dude, I think Mim ate all my candy," Warner said, shaking his head. "All I have left now is some stuff to make s'mores and a case of energy cola under the bed."

"Look on the bright side," said Kevin. "If Mim hadn't eaten it all, we'd be totally busted right now, and we could kiss our chances at the Invention Convention good-bye. You kind of owe him one."

A few moments later, Tara radioed in on the walkie-talkie. "Hey, guys, come in. Over."

Kevin picked up the call. "Hey, Tara."

"Mim's ready for us out in the woods."

"We'll meet you there. Just give us five minutes to ditch robotics lab. Over."

They crept into the forest, weaving between the tree trunks. Long diagonal shafts of sunlight shone down through the leaves and branches overhead. As they reached the clearing in the middle of the woods, the wilderness took on an eerie quiet. The faint buzz of mosquitoes played under the light breeze rustling through the treetops.

Kevin, Tara, Warner, and TJ sat on one of the picnic benches near a fire pit, facing Mim, who stood illuminated in a bright triangular sunbeam.

"Lady and gentlemen, you're about to get the ultimate crash course in alien self-defense," Mim said, gesturing with his arms as he spoke. "Before I start"—he turned to Warner—"do you have any more of those delicious foodstuffs?"

"No, thanks to you," Warner replied, narrowing his eyes at the little purple alien. "Look, Mim, I don't know how you do things on planet wherever-you're-from, but on planet Earth, eating someone's entire candy stash without asking is not cool."

"Take a chill pill, Warner," Tara piped up. "You've been overcharging me for Drake's Coffee Cakes all summer."

"It's my fault, you guys," Mim said. "Sometimes my appetite gets the best of me."

"That's okay, man," Warner said. "We're still boys."

"Now let's get down to business." Mim opened his black alien space bag and laid out the contents on the ground.

Kevin recognized the first alien gadget as the freeze ray Mim had zapped Alexander with. Next to it was another device that looked like a metallic sombrero. A pair of jet-black mittens made out of a shiny plastic-looking material lay beside a silver disc shaped like a hockey puck, with a sparkly gemstone attached to the center. The last contraption looked like a watch band with a handgrip that jutted out where the face of the watch would be. On the handgrip shimmered a few control buttons and a lens that looked like a prism. Mim picked up the strange and beautiful gemstone hockey puck first and held it out in the palm of his hand. "This, friends, is what you might call a shrink ray," he said, and then took his hand away. The shrink ray hovered in the air on its own for a moment before it sprouted three mechanical legs and stood up like a tripod. One of Mim's other arms then reached out and pressed a button on the side of the disk, and a horseshoe-shaped screen rose from the flat surface of the disk. "Check this out. This one's easy."

They stood behind the shrink ray as Mim showed them the controls on the U-shaped touchscreen. On the left of the screen, a high-definition video image showed the landscape in front of them. "First

you must pick a target." Mim touched his finger to the screen and highlighted a big rock on the ground. "Then you select the percent minimization and hit this icon here." He tapped a small but- 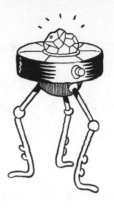 ton on the screen, and the gemstone started to glow a deep shade of red. A second later, the alien crystal emitted a long and perfectly straight laser beam aimed directly at the rock. A bright light flashed, and Kevin blinked. When his eyes opened and regained focus in the daylight, the rock had become a tiny pebble.

"No way!" Warner said excitedly.

"Yes way," said Mim. "I'm sure you can see this can be a very dangerous device, so be careful."

"What's this weird hat?" Tara asked, turning her attention to the next piece of alien technology set out on the forest floor.

"Go ahead," said Mim. "Try it on."

"What does it do?"

"It's a telepathy helmet. Lets you read and control someone else's mind," the furry little alien said. "One of a kind."

Tara put on the helmet. The alien headpiece looked like a mix between a flying saucer and a sombrero. As soon as she set the contraption on top of her head, a visor came down in front of her eyes and two earplugs dangled from the sides.

Mim instructed her to put the earplugs in her ears and then hit a large, rubbery button on its brim. The telepathy helmet sparkled to life. "Now, look at Warner and ask him anything you want to know. But Warner, only answer in your mind, not out loud."

"Umm, okay," Tara said. "What's the most embarrassing thing that's happened to you in the last year?"

Warner closed his eyes, thinking, and a long silence followed.

"OMG," Tara said, lifting up the visor on the telepathy helmet. "You wet the bed?"

"Hey! No, I don't . . . I mean, I was trying not to think of that."

"Gross," she said. "I just saw a little memory clip. He was at camp. It was, like, two weeks ago."

"Aw, man," Kevin said. "Glad I'm on the top bunk."

"Ha ha," said Warner. "Very funny."

"All right, all right, no more telepathy helmet for now," Mim said, taking the contraption off Tara's head.

Mim turned his attention to the next alien gadget lying on the forest floor.

"This baby right here is what's known as a wormhole generator," said Mim. "It can teleport its chosen target to any point in the galaxy."

The kids kept nodding, listening intently.

"The device is linked up to an interstellar network of wormholes in over one hundred inhabited planets across the Milky Way galaxy. All you have to do is select a destination, turn on the infrared molecular oscillator, and watch the portal whirl your target to another world. It can come in real handy if there's someone after you who you don't want to be after you anymore."

"Can you use it on yourself?" TJ asked.

"I've never tried," said Mim. "But I wouldn't recommend it. You Earthlings wouldn't fare too well out there." He gestured to the cosmos, then continued. "Last but not least, these are the positron force-field gloves. Who wants to try?"

Kevin jumped forward, and Mim handed him the gloves. Kevin slipped them on, and Mim showed him the power button located on the wristband. He hit the switch and the gloves charged up. Kevin's hands felt lighter than air.

"Now hold both of your hands about a foot in front of your face, palms facing outward." Mim stood directly in front of Kevin, then scooped up a sizable rock from the forest floor and launched it on a line right at Kevin's head. Kevin didn't even have time to flinch.

PING!

The rock glanced off the force field into the air, which shimmered like a mirage and rippled as if it were liquid. The rock then ricocheted off a hollow part of a tree and landed close by.

"Whoa!" Kevin, Warner, Tara, and TJ all exclaimed.

"Glad you like my goodies," said Mim. "We shouldn't play around with these too much. We'll need every bit of power if more aliens come after me, but it's important for you to know how to use them."

PING!

"Thanks for teaching us about all this stuff, Mim," said TJ. "As far as we're concerned, this is like the coolest thing ever."

"You're welcome," said the little alien. "But you guys are the ones doing me a favor. Let me know if there's anything I can do for you in return."

"Actually, it would be really cool if you could help us out with something," said Kevin.

"Anything you want," said Mim.

"We've got that thing at three o'clock tomorrow," Kevin said. "The Invention Convention. It's real important to us."

"Kevin," said Tara. "Are you sure that's a good idea?"

"What do you mean?" Kevin said. "We need him to prove the galactascope works. That's why we brought him here, I mean, ya know, aside from making a new friend and all."

"Aha, I get it, I get it," said Mim. "I would be happy to help you win your contest."

"Mim," said Kevin. "You're the best, dude. Really,

you don't know what this means."

"I wouldn't miss it for the world," said Mim. He then plucked a fat summer spider off its web and popped the bug into his mouth.

The next day the air was abuzz with massive swarms of mosquitoes as Kevin, Warner, and TJ rolled their galactascope through camp and stopped outside the gymnasium, where the Invention Convention would be held that afternoon. They had covered the galactascope with a spare bedsheet to hide it from any prying eyes.

With only an hour or so before the convention, Kevin couldn't help feeling a little anxious, even though he knew their walking, talking alien was going to blow Alexander and his hovercraft out of the water.

"Ugh," said Kevin, smacking one of the little bloodsuckers into a red splotch on his arm. "We gotta tell Mim to stop eating so many spiders."

"Yeah," said Warner. "By the way, where is the little purple spider eater?"

"Tara said she was going to pick him up from the shed," said TJ.

"Okay, cool," Kevin said. "I just want to walk him through our presentation before the convention." He pulled out the walkie-talkie and pressed the call button. "Tara. You with Mim? Over."

A few seconds later, Tara's voice came through the receiver. "I can't find him," her voice crackled. "He's not with you guys?"

"Wait, what do you mean you can't find him?" Kevin was starting to get worried. If they didn't have an alien to show, they had no proof that their invention actually worked.

"I'll check the shed again," Tara promised.

"Let's split up. TJ, you check the bunk. Warner, check the mess hall, and I'll check the labs," said Kevin. "Tara, if he's not in the shed, you check the forest. We'll report back here in one hour."

An hour later, Kevin waited for his teammates outside the field house, kicking the dirt. Kevin had searched the camp high and low, but Mim was nowhere to be found.

A few minutes passed and Warner, TJ, and Tara approached, looking down in the dumps. Kevin started to realize this was about to be the worst Invention Convention ever.

"You guys," said Kevin, "what are we going to do? Without Mim, this thing is useless. No one's going to believe we were talking to a real live alien unless we can show them a real live alien!"

Warner slapped his hand down on Kevin's shoulder. "Whether we win or not, *you* know that we did something incredible, so that's all that matters. Even though that trip to Hawaii would have been really cool."

"I guess you're right," Kevin said, trying to calm his nerves. He just couldn't believe that he was going to lose to Alexander once again.

Kevin accepted defeat as the Extraordinary Terrestrials made their way into the field house, but before they could enter the convention, the Vainglorious Math Nerds strolled by. Kevin squinted coldly as he and Alexander locked eyes. Without breaking his glare, Alexander sneered and dragged his index finger across the width of his neck.

Doing his best to ignore his nemesis, Kevin pushed past him and led the way into the gymnasium, while Warner and TJ rolled their now useless galactascope in behind him. Setting their invention off to the side, they climbed the bleachers and took their seats in the crowd, waiting for the convention to begin.

Camp Director Dimpus made his way onto the stage

and raised his arms to signal the crowd to simmer down. "Welcome to this year's Invention Convention! Thank you all for participating. It's been an amazing summer so far, and I've had the privilege of witnessing some of the most impressive creative thinking and dedicated work in all my twenty years at this camp. Before me sits a fine collection of young scientific minds, and I know you're all excited to see what your fellow campers have invented. So without further ado: may the best scientists win." The crowd applauded, and Dimpus introduced the first team.

As Alexander had told them, Team Quasar had

indeed developed a formula for a kind of soda pop that turned the drinker's hair purple. Using one of their team-mates as a test subject, they demonstrated the effect of the soda. Kevin watched as their teammate guzzled the fizzy beverage, and within a few seconds, his light-blond hair magically turned a dark shade of purple.

Time couldn't have gone slow enough. Maybe Mim was still running on his old planet's time. Maybe three o'clock here was like thirteen o'clock there. It didn't mat-ter. The Invention Convention had already begun, and Mim was a no-show. Kevin's stomach fell and his chest

tightened. He couldn't believe that after everything, Mim had really bailed on him.

All he could do was sit back and observe as others qualified to win the prize and stature that was rightfully his. Kevin had to admit, though, there were some other pretty cool inventions this year.

One group had created a filtration system that could reuse and purify bath and shower water for future baths and showers, which Kevin thought was good for the environment, but also kind of gross. Another team had built a robot that cleaned and did other basic chores. And another had made a superstrong bike helmet that looked identical to a baseball cap.

Then it was Alexander's turn. The lights in the gymnasium dimmed.

His hovercraft lit up and rose off the court as Alexander spoke from the cockpit, holding a wireless microphone. "I decided to design this hovercraft after getting cut from my seventh-grade B team in basketball. I'm sure many of us have felt that same pain and humiliation. But I knew I could do something those

basketball-dribbling jocks couldn't. Ladies and gentle-men: I give you the HoverTron."

The hovercraft flew about seven feet off the ground. Alexander steered it over the free-throw line, facing one of the hoops in the auditorium, where Dante and Luke were waiting beneath him with a rack of basketballs that they began to toss in the air. Alexander's hovercraft floated toward the rim, and he caught three consecutive alley-oops from his buddies, dunking the balls like an NBA superstar.

The camp broke out in a thunderous applause, everyone except Kevin, Warner, TJ, and Tara, who sat there with their heads in their hands. Alexander locked eyes with Kevin again and winked, blowing him an obnoxious little kiss.

Kevin caught Alexander's air kiss and threw it to the ground, stomping it with his foot as he stood up. The Extraordinary Terrestrials were up next, and Kevin walked to the stage with his friends. He cleared his throat, preparing to explain that they had nothing to show, when Tara interrupted him.

"Fellow campers," she said, pushing her way in front and unzipping the backpack she was wearing, "we, the Extraordinary Terrestrials, will now demonstrate the great power of the human mind by using this invention, which my team and I have dubbed the Telepathy Helmet." She lifted the alien headgear out of the bag with a flourish. "For this, I'll need a volunteer."

A few hands in the audience shot up, including Alexander, who stood quickly and said, "I'll do it."

"Yes," said Tara. "You will make an excellent guinea pig, Mr. Russ."

"Dude," Kevin said, nudging Warner in the rib cage. "What is she doing? That's not ours. We didn't invent that."

Alexander sat down at the card table on the stage across from Tara. "This ought to be good for a laugh," he said.

"Please allow me a moment while I make some preliminary predictions." She placed the alien helmet on her head and activated the power source. The brain-wave sensors on the crown of the headpiece rotated around, gathering subconscious data from Alexander's mind.

"Mr. Russ," Tara continued her psychic lady routine, "I'm going to need your utmost focus."

Alexander rolled his eyes as Tara pulled on the telepathy helmet and the visor lowered in front of her eyes automatically. "Whoa," she said out of the blue, and then looked up at her subject.

"Been having some strange dreams lately, Mr. Russ?"

Alexander glared at her suspiciously and chuckled.

"Don't we all? The average human dreams about fifteen hundred times a year. That's 4.10958 dreams a night, for those of you who can't divide in their heads."

"That's 4.09836 on a leap year," she retorted calmly.

"Yeah, yeah," Alexander said. "Let's just get on with this charade so I can collect my blue ribbon."

"Very well," Tara said. "We shall see." She ignored him and continued the demonstration. TJ then appeared next to Alexander, holding a pair of swimming goggles with black tape blocking out the clear plastic lenses. "Please allow my assistant to blindfold you for this demonstration."

"Whatever you say, lady." Alexander crossed his arms, and TJ put the goggles on him.

"Mr. Russ," Tara said with utter politeness, "now would you be so kind as to think of three words? Be sure to think of three really hard words no one but you would ever be able to guess." As Alexander thought silently, Tara took out three pieces of paper and began to scribble something down on each sheet, then handed them over to TJ.

"Now," she said. "Say the first word aloud."

TJ was already behind Alexander, holding up the predicted word written on the paper for the audience to see. It said: ECTOPLASM.

"Ectoplasm," Alexander said, still blindfolded. The crowd gasped, and everyone held their breath. "Now say the second," she said.

TJ shuffled to the next piece of paper. It read: BARF FACE.

"Well," said Alexander, "it's actually two words, but the words are barf face."

"And lastly," Tara said.

"Scrumdiddlyumptious," Alexander said.

TJ held up the final sheet of paper, which read: SCRUMDIDDLYUMPTIOUS.

The crowd sat in silence for a moment and then ripped up in applause.

Alexander tore off the blindfold to see the last word he had thought of written on the paper.

"This is nothing more than a parlor trick!" he shouted. "You'll need more than a few lucky guesses to convince me."

"All right then, you'll stay for one more demonstration," Tara said. "Now, Mr. Russ, would you please let your mind go blank? I'm going to perform a bit of hypnotism."

"Oh, please. You think you can hypnotize this guy?" He pointed to himself with both thumbs. "Give it your best shot."

Tara reactivated the visor on the telepathy helmet, and the brain-wave sensors started to rotate and focus in Alexander's direction. The field house grew silent. Kevin held his breath for a few seconds before Alexander rose from his chair, tucked his hands under his armpits, and started to flap his elbows as if they were wings.

"Bawk-bawk-bawk." Alexander began to cluck like a chicken and strut around. "Bawk-bawk-bawk!"

All the campers burst into laughter, even Luke and Dante, who couldn't help but chuckle. After Tara let Alexander walk around and cluck for a good ten seconds, the nerd bully sat back down and came out of the hypnosis as if nothing had happened.

"I'm still waiting," he said, tapping his foot with his arms crossed.

The entire camp burst into applause, hooting and hollering.

"I don't get it!" Alexander stood up. "What are you all cheering for?"

The whole camp swarmed the presentation area and lifted Tara up off the ground and onto their shoulders, all cheering for the high-tech feat of other-worldly magic. "Hooray!"

Kevin, Warner, and TJ were right there helping her crowd-surf, holding her up by the backs of her knees. Tara giggled down at Kevin, who looked up and shook his head with a knowing smile. "That was incredible!" he shouted with a sudden jolt of laughter. "This is crazy!"

"Tara! Tara!" the campers shouted in rhythm with one another.

TWEEEEET! Dimpus blew his whistle and shouted, "Order!" The campers set Tara back down on the floor and hushed up, all except for Alexander, who kept right on shouting at the top of his lungs.

"What a joke! What a sham! What a hoax!" he hollered over the quiet whir of the mosquito swarms buzzing through the gymnasium.

"Alexander!" Dimpus raised his voice to a sharp bark. "Settle down—"

"I will not settle down, sir, until these imposters are exposed!"

As Alexander's face flushed red, one of the campers who had been recording the telepathy helmet demonstration came forward and showed Alexander the video.

Alexander snatched the phone and looked at the playback.

"I don't get it. How did you make me . . . ?" His voice trailed off, defeated. Alexander's eyes glazed over as he began to mumble, which quickly turned into babbling. "It's gotta be the aliens. The aliens are real!"

"Aliens?" Dimpus raised one skeptical eyebrow.

"The ones in my dream," said Alexander. "The aliens made me think it was a dream, but it was real. It's diabolical!" He snarled viciously and pointed at the Extraordinary Terrestrials. "They're the ones. They're in league with the aliens! That's how they got the technology! The aliens gave it to them. They might even be alien clones!" His voice cracked as he ran out of breath.

Suddenly, Miss Mackenzie, the camp nurse, appeared next to Alexander and took him by the arm. "There, there, Alexander," she said in a soothing tone. "Let's go get you some ice cream and a cool washcloth to put on your forehead."

"Ice cream?" Alexander's voice was like an excited child's. "I love ice cream."

"I know you do," the nurse said, leading him off to the infirmary.

Now that every group had presented their inventions Dimpus walked up to the Extraordinary Terrestrials. "Hovercrafts . . . telepathy helmets . . . soda that makes your hair turn different colors. This is going to be a tough one to judge. You'll have my verdict tomorrow." Dimpus laughed to himself. "You kids are going to take over the world someday. What's under there?" Dimpus asked, turning his attention to the galactascope, which was sitting under the sheet off to the side.

"Oh, nothing," Kevin said. "Just some other project that didn't really work out."

As the camp director walked off, Warner punched Kevin in the shoulder as hard as he could.

"Dude!" Warner said, hugging his pal. "We totally just won the Invention Convention!"

"We'll find out tomorrow, I guess," Kevin said, looking a little glum.

"Cheer up, Kev," TJ said, patting his friend on the back. "Even if we don't win, we still made Alexander squawk like a big chicken."

Kevin cracked a half smile. He was still a little bummed about Mim, but TJ was right. It was pretty funny.

"Pretty funny?" said a little voice in his head. "It was hilarious!"

Kevin looked over at Tara, who had put the telepathy helmet back on and was aiming it at him. "Will you take that thing off already and get out of my head? Jeez!"

Kevin and the gang strolled back to the bunks after dinner. Everyone at camp was chattering about how awesome this year's Invention Convention was, especially the telepathy helmet. But Kevin didn't feel like celebrating. He kicked the dirt in frustration and made a grumbling sound.

"What's the matter, man?" Warner asked. "You still upset about Mim's no-show?"

"I just didn't think he would do that," said Kevin. "He promised me! He promised us!" Immediately he heard how whiny his voice sounded. "Never mind."

"It's probably for the best, Kev," said Tara. "It would

have been pretty risky anyway."

"Yeah," TJ said. "If we'd unveiled a real live alien, it would have been all over the news. A bunch of government dudes could have come and taken Mim away."

"Not to mention the space poachers could have intercepted the transmissions," added Tara.

"I guess you're right," Kevin said. "I haven't been able to think straight since we started working on the IC. I just wanted to beat Alexander so bad."

"Well, guess what, buddy?" Warner said. "That's exactly what we did."

"Not yet," Kevin said. "And we didn't even get to do it with our own invention. Don't you guys feel like we cheated a little bit?"

"Maybe we didn't invent the telepathy helmet," Warner said. "But we created the galactascope, which brought us the alien that brought us the helmet."

"Yeah, I guess so," Kevin said. "But it's not the same."

"Bottom line, man," TJ said. "We made Alexander cluck like a chicken in front of the entire camp."

Kevin chuckled. "That was pretty funny, huh?"

"Okay, boys," Tara said, walking off toward her bunk. "I'm gonna go chill out for a little bit. Hit me up on the walkie-talkie if anything's going on."

"See you later, Tara!" the boys called out as she strolled away.

Kevin opened the door to their cabin, and the boys looked down at the floor. The place was a mess. Mim was scrambling around frantically, picking things up

and throwing them over his shoulder. The fluffy, purple-furred alien turned to them with hysteria in his eyes. "Where's the telepathy helmet?"

"Umm," said TJ. "We kind of had to borrow it."

"You what?"

"We needed it for the Invention Convention," Warner said. "Because *you* didn't show."

"Okay," he said. "I'm just glad to know you have it. If that device fell into the wrong hands, it could have terrible consequences."

"Well," said Kevin. "Next time you're gonna flake out, could you let us know ahead of time?"

"I'm sorry, I'm sorry, I know I messed up," said Mim. "But I had a terrible feeling the trackers were getting closer, and I couldn't risk being out in the open. For all we know, they could already be here."

Just then Mim groaned and doubled over in pain, clutching his stomach.

"You okay?" Warner asked.

"Just hunger pains. I get them sometimes," said Mim. "You got anything to eat?"

"All I have are these s'mores ingredients," Warner replied.

"What's a s'more?" Mim asked.

"I'll show you outside," said Warner. "Hey, TJ, do you think you could use your Boy Scouting skills to start up a bonfire for us?"

"Sure," said TJ. "We've got an hour before curfew."

"Great," said Warner. "We need to refuel, especially if those poachers are on their way."

"Yeah, we deserve it," said Kevin, starting to forgive Mim a little. "Lemme call Tara."

Together, Kevin, Warner, TJ, Tara, and Mim ducked into the thicket of trees leading into the dark pine forest. They were each wearing backpacks carrying s'more supplies and Mim's stash of alien defense gadgets, just in case he was right. Kevin was even feeling excited to show Mim one of the all-time best things about being human: melted chocolate and gooey marshmallows sandwiched between two graham crackers.

After TJ started up the fire in the pit, the red-and-orange glow of the flames flickered across their faces as they found suitable sticks and branches for roasting their marshmallows.

"I like mine burnt," Kevin said, stabbing a marshmallow onto his roasting stick and holding it over the fire.

"Yuck, that's nasty," said Tara. "I like mine nice and golden brown."

"Why do they call them s'mores?" Mim asked, adding two extra marshmallows to his stick.

"Because once you have a taste, you have to have some more," Warner said.

They roasted the marshmallows over the flames and when they were done, Warner raised his marshmallow-roasting stick into the air. "To Mim," Warner said, toasting their alien buddy. "If it weren't for you, we never would have beaten Alexander."

"Yee-yah," said TJ, high-fiving Mim.

"Hear, hear," said Kevin, finally getting into the spirit. He raised his charbroiled marshmallow out of the fire and into the air. "To Mim!"

Mim mimicked Kevin and toasted them all with his marshmallow stick. "To all of you. If it weren't for you, I wouldn't be here to celebrate today."

"Cheers to that," Tara said as they began to sandwich their marshmallows onto the graham crackers and chocolate.

"MMMMMM." Mim chewed his first-ever bite of s'more. "This is the greatest thing I've ever tasted. Gimme some more s'more." He gobbled the rest of it down and immediately started fixing more with all his arms, roasting four marshmallows at the same time.

Kevin stuffed a large hunk of chocolate marshmallowy goodness into his mouth and closed his eyes to savor the bite. He swallowed and opened his eyes, tilting his head back. He looked up to the sky and nearly choked at the sight overhead.

A large, triangular-shaped spacecraft hovered silently just above the treetops.

Then it disappeared as if cloaked with some kind of invisibility shield.

Kevin rubbed his eyes. "Did you guys just see that?" he asked.

"See what?" Tara murmured with a mouthful of chocolate marshmallow.

"I thought I just saw—"

"What's that?" TJ said, turning his head toward the thicket of trees behind them. Kevin heard it too, the footsteps crunching and cracking.

"Aha!" Cody said as he, Nick, and Bailey stepped into the clearing. "Here they are!"

"What are you doing out here this late?" Bailey

asked. "You guys had us worried sick!"

"What the heck is that thing?" Nick asked, pointing at Mim, who was scarfing down his fourth or fifth s'more.

Before they could answer, three large, bulky figures rappelled from the treetops. *ZHWOOP! ZHWOOP! ZHWOOP!* The trio of alien bonfire crashers hit the ground with a *thunk* that shook the earth and detached from their drop lines.

One of the aliens looked like a giant slug sitting on top of a set of six crab legs. Its mouth ran like a Mohawk over the top of its head, and its eyes were attached to long antennae sprouting off the side of its face. The nasty-looking alien had four arms with sharp claws jutting out from the wrists. The other two aliens were cast in the shadows, but the massive four-armed slug-crab moved forward into the flickering light of the bonfire.

Nick, Cody, and Bailey all dropped their jaws.

"Whoa," Cody said.

"Sweet," Nick echoed.

"Kevin," said Bailey. "What's going on?"

Kevin watched in horror as the slug alien pulled out a large plasma ray and aimed it at the counselors.

ZAP! ZAP! The alien unleashed two shots, and Nick and Cody froze, encased in some type of clear cocoon. *ZAP!* One more quick shot nailed Bailey with the same effect, immobilizing him as if he were trapped in a block of ice.

Mim's eyes widened as he stopped gorging himself on the s'mores and jumped to his feet. "Run!"

Kevin, Warner, Tara, TJ, and Mim took off in different directions, sprinting for their lives as two more aliens dropped out of the sky.

THUMP-THUMP! ZAP! A bright-white blast of light shot out from the crab-legged slug beast's plasma ray. *ZAP! ZAP!* Two more blasts followed and nearly struck Mim as he raced for cover in the forest.

Mim bounded up the side of a tree trunk and leaped to grab one of the low-hanging branches to dodge the double blob of paralyzing plasma heading right for him. *ZAP!* Mim swung and launched himself into the air as the fourth laser-ray blast whizzed past and singed off a patch of his purple fur.

A loaded silence suddenly fell over the woods. Kevin ducked behind a tree as Mim disappeared into the foliage, still swinging from branch to branch. Kevin looked around frantically, his head moving like it was on a swivel, but he had already lost track of his friends in the chaos, and his asthma was starting to act up in the panic. He tried to control his breathing, but he felt his lungs tighten with each and every breath. Kevin sucked back a puff of his inhaler and held it in for a two-count before exhaling slowly.

The sound of footsteps scuttled behind him, crunching and crackling through the bracken. Someone was on his tail. "Warner? Tara?" he called out in a strained whisper.

ZAP! ZAP! Two more alien laser blasts shattered a tree branch above Kevin's head. He covered his face with both his arms and sprinted away in a shower of splintered bark.

THUMP! THUMP! THUMP! The alien footsteps picked up their pace. Kevin glanced over his shoulder. Big mistake! The alien hunter was even bigger than he thought. Just over seven feet tall, Kevin guesstimated.

Its bulbous eyes were set wide apart on either side of its head where its temples should have been. A wedge of tough-looking dinosaur-like flesh came down the middle of its forehead like a widow's peak. Portions of its arms and legs seemed to be made entirely out of metal, as if the alien was hardwired with some kind of advanced biomechanics. Around its right shiny black eyeball, a patch of computerized circuitry was embedded and fused to the extraterrestrial's skin. The giant half-cyborg space beast grunted once, then paused for a moment, breathing loudly through its wide mouth, which stretched across the entire lower part of its chinless face and was filled with jagged double rows of small, pointy teeth.

Thinking quickly, Kevin picked up a large rock off

the ground. He looked down the narrow footpath leading through the woods back to camp and chucked the
stone the opposite way. The stone ricocheted off a tree
trunk with a hollow *thunk*. The humongous alien flipped
its robotic gaze toward the noise, and Kevin took off running in the other direction.

He raced out of the dark woodland and sped across
the campgrounds, making a beeline for the first building he saw: the field house.

At the door, Kevin unzipped his bag and pulled out
the positron force-field gloves
from underneath the
shrink ray at the bottom
of the backpack.

He looked back
toward the forest as
he put on the alien
defense gloves. The
half-cyborg ET tracker
emerged from the
woods. A hint of

moonlight glinted off its metallic pieces as the space hunter walked briskly toward Kevin with purpose.

Kevin activated the positron force field, turning the power up full blast. He wasn't about to get zapped by some half-robot alien freak.

He cranked his arm back and then heaved his gloved hand toward the door like a karate master punching from the hip. The lock on the door broke from the otherworldly force, and in a flash Kevin was inside the field house, running up the steps leading to the basketball court.

He hustled through the double doors to the gymnasium, passing by the wall lined with all the inventions from the convention that day. In the shadowy gym, Kevin stood up on his tippy toes and peered through the small square window on one of the doors. He held his breath as he saw the enormous cyborg space poacher turn the corner of the hallway and pause for a moment, looking toward the gymnasium doors.

Kevin sank down quickly so as not to be seen. *I'm too young to die,* he thought. *I haven't even won the Nobel*

Prize yet! Kevin backed away from the entrance and crouched underneath a table to the left of the door.

The place was dark except for the faint light coming in through the windows, which illuminated Alexander's hovercraft across from him.

Kevin removed his force-field gloves and took the shrink ray out from his backpack. He held the alien gadget in the palm of his hand and pressed the button to flip it open. The horseshoe-shaped touch screen elevated off the puck-sized disk as the shrink ray sparked to life, glowing in the darkness. The tripod legs unfolded automatically and hit the floor, stabilizing the device just under the tabletop.

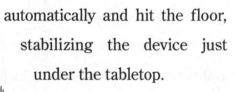

From outside the doors, a loud clanking noise echoed down the halls. Kevin's face turned almost blue in the long, breathless silence that followed. He wished he were wearing the telepathy helmet so he might know the alien's next move, but they had left that back at the bunk.

BOOM! The double doors burst open with such a force that they flew off the hinges and slid to the center of the basketball court. Kevin froze, but his heart was still beating at sixty miles per hour as the massive space poacher stepped slowly into the gymnasium.

Although Kevin was safe beneath the table, he could see the cyborg alien's weaponry on the shrink ray's high-def video display. Kevin hit the same settings Mim had shown them in the forest the day before, making the extraterrestrial gemstone laser glow a dark red and then beam a thin, straight laser from the precious alien stone. Kevin trained the ray directly on the alien's leg muscle and pressed the button.

The shrink ray flashed like a camera, but before the laser beam made it across the gym, the cyborg alien jumped out of its path. The shrink ray's beam instead landed on Alexander's hovercraft, shrinking it down to the size of a remote-controlled car.

Shoot, Kevin thought, focusing his attention back on the touch screen. He watched the alien's reaction on the video interface.

The cyborg looked around for the source of the laser, its rock-solid arm held out, ready to aim right at Kevin.

Kevin hurriedly selected the alien's figure on the screen again and hit the shrink button.

The red, glowing gemstone shot another laser beam, which landed this time on the alien cyborg's hip.

Direct hit! In a flash the mammoth alien shrank to the size of a Barbie doll. Kevin let out a little whoop and stood up from under the table. He towered over the shrunken cyborg, which didn't look as scary anymore. The little alien swiveled his head about, disoriented, pointing his ray-gun arm all over the place. Finally he caught his bearings and looked up to see Kevin, the giant thirteen-year-old. The dwarfed alien aimed his arm up and fired his phaser weapon, striking Kevin on the shin.

"Hey, stop that," Kevin said. "That tickles!"

The miniaturized alien ceased fire and lowered his

shooting arm. "What have you done to me?" The alien spoke in perfect English.

He must have one of those language chips, Kevin thought.

The mini cyborg continued, "How am I supposed to catch Mim now?"

"He's an endangered species," Kevin scolded him. "You ought to be ashamed of yourself!"

"You must be confused," said the alien. "Who are you? Identify yourself."

"You first, dude," Kevin said. "What's your name?"

"My name is Klyk," the miniature alien said. "I work

for the Interplanetary Peace Coalition."

"What? So you're like some kind of space cop?"

"More of a bounty hunter," said Klyk. "I help them track down the galaxy's most wanted criminals."

"Huh?" Kevin said. "You think Mim's a criminal?"

"See for yourself," said Klyk as he pulled out a tiny device from his belt. He clicked a button, and a beam of light projected a holograph into the air. A 3D image of Mim's mug shot appeared in front of Kevin. Lists of data streamed down on either side of his face, illustrating his entire criminal profile. Master of deception. Intergalactic tech thief. Known planet eater. A long list of Mim's partners in crime followed, which read like an unsolved word jumble.

Kevin's eyes went wide and unblinking as he examined the holographic rap sheet. "I don't know what to say. . . . I mean, I thought he was our friend."

"Just how well do you know this Mim?" asked Klyk.

"We only met him a few days ago," said Kevin. "He told us you guys were space poachers trying to hunt him down for his fur."

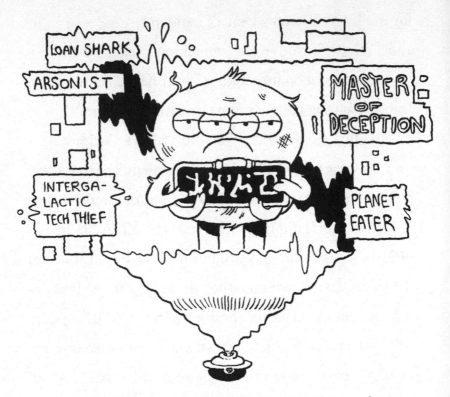

"And you believed that?" Klyk raised his eyebrows.

"Well, yeah!" said Kevin, looking a little crestfallen. "Aw, man, I feel like such an idiot!"

"Don't feel too bad. Mim's the galactic champion of liars," said Klyk. "He's wanted for the destruction of five entire planets across the galaxy. I've been ordered by the council to bring him in, dead or alive."

Kevin could hardly believe what Klyk was saying.

But then he thought of Mim's eating habits, and it all made sense.

"Wait," said Kevin. "We have to find Tara, Warner, and TJ before your partners hurt them! They still think Mim's a good guy."

Kevin scooped up the miniaturized alien, tossed him in his backpack, and bolted back into the night.

Kevin raced outside, looking around for his friends. His eyes darted from the lakeshore to the mess hall and back again. A series of bright, quick flashes caught his attention, and he turned his gaze toward the edge of the forest.

Kevin ran toward the spot and ducked into the pinewoods.

Two alien photon blasts shot through the darkness and whizzed past Kevin's head. Sprinting with both arms shielding his skull, Kevin dove and slid like a base runner into a shallow ditch behind a few large evergreen trees.

He looked to his left and saw two of Klyk's bounty hunter pals maneuvering cautiously through the forest. Kevin recognized one of them as the half-slug, half-crab alien centaur that had zapped the counselors. The extra-terrestrial next to it was equally as revolting. Its face was like a giant squid, with squiggly tentacles wriggling off its chin like a beard made of snakes. It had no torso, just a long neck sprouting out of its waist. It stood on two legs with backward-bending knee joints, and three arms protruded from its waist, two off the hips and one out from the tailbone.

There were two more aliens on the prowl about twenty yards away from them. Kevin squinted his eyes through the darkness to catch a glimpse. Both alien bounty hunters were identical to each other: large insectoids that if Kevin wasn't mistaken resembled assassin bugs. Except these assassin bugs were both about six feet tall and walked on their hind legs. Long snouts protruded like elephants' trunks, and long antennae pointed up from the top of their heads.

Kevin was about to ask Klyk for help when he looked to the right and saw his friends jump out from behind a row of bushes.

Warner thrust his arm forward, wearing the wormhole generator. "Hah! Take that!"

The two alien assassin bugs spun around and were suddenly stunned, backlit in a bright, swirling green light. Within seconds, their silhouettes disappeared as if they'd been sucked into a point the size of a pinhole.

Warner whirled around and activated the wormhole generator again as the squid-faced alien and the crab-legged blobbermouth came bounding toward him down the footpath.

"Warner, no!" Kevin shouted, running toward his friends. "Don't!"

But it was too late. The alien bounty-hunting duo had already vanished into the wormhole too.

"Boom! Did you see that?" Warner said, pumping his fist. "I just sent those suckers to another dimension. Four for the price of two! What!"

Kevin clutched his forehead and wiped the sweat gathering at his brow. "Oh man, this is so not good!"

"You're dang right it wasn't good," Warner said. "It was freakin' unbelievable."

"You guys," said Tara. "Mim's still out there. I think I saw them shoot him. He could be hurt!"

Before Kevin could respond, the zipper on his backpack seemed to open on its own and Klyk climbed out. He walked up Kevin's arm and stood on his shoulder like a parrot. "We can only hope," Klyk said from his perch.

Warner, Tara, and TJ simultaneously dropped their jaws at the sight of the toy-sized alien.

"Whoa," said Warner. "Kevin, you shrank a space poacher!"

TJ ran his index finger along the top of Klyk's head. "Hey, boy."

"Hands off." Klyk batted Warner's finger away and looked up at Kevin.

"He's not a space poacher, guys," said Kevin. "Mim's been lying to us the whole time."

"What are you talking about?" Warner said.

"I can't explain here," Klyk spoke. "But Mim is not your friend. We need to get inside immediately. It's not safe out here with Mim on the loose."

Back at the boys' bunk, the Extraordinary Terrestrials formed a circle around their new alien ally. They all listened intently as Klyk pulled out his miniaturized 3D hologram gadget and filled them in on the truth about Mim.

"You have no idea what Mim is capable of. If left to his own devices, Mim could destroy Earth in a matter of days. Maybe less. I'm the only one left who can capture him, and you've reduced me to this."

"Man," said Tara. "I really thought Mim was our buddy."

"Why don't you just call for some backup and we can all lie low for a hot second while we wait for the cavalry," Warner said.

"I would, but my radio is now also shrunken and useless. No signal."

"What do we do then?" Kevin asked. "There's no one else coming?"

"No," said Klyk. "The five of us were the only ones they sent. The best, supposedly."

"The guys who met their match against a bunch of science geeks were the best you got?" Warner asked.

"Children aren't usually armed with advanced alien technology," said Klyk. "Now let me think. There's a chance Zeff might still be on the way."

"Zeff?" Kevin said. "Was he a really big insect guy with a robot suit?"

"What do you mean, 'was'?" Klyk asked.

"Umm," said TJ, butting in. "Mim kind of blasted him away with that de-atomizer ray thingamajig."

"He de-atomized Zeff?" Klyk said, hanging his head solemnly.

"Yeah," said Tara. "We thought Zeff was trying to kill Mim."

"Well, Mim *was* Zeff's mortal enemy," said Klyk.

"Mim ate Zeff's entire planet. Zeff was the only one who escaped, and he vowed to track Mim down to get his revenge."

The kids sat for a minute in the late night quiet before the miniaturized alien crime fighter spoke again.

"You need to tell me as much about Mim's behavior as you can," Klyk said.

"Like what?" Tara asked.

"Has he been eating?" said Klyk.

"Are you kidding? That's all he does," Warner said. "He ate all my candy."

"He ate all the spiders, too," TJ added. "Why?"

"The more Mim eats, the hungrier he gets," Klyk said with a grave face. "He starts off small and then moves on to much bigger things." He paused for a moment, scratching his head. "What about the gear?" Klyk continued. "You seem to be equipped with the most state-of-the-art alien self-defense machines. Does Mim have anything?"

"Uh . . . ," Kevin said. "He might still have that thing he used to vaporize Zeff."

"It looked like a big lightsaber," Warner added.

"It's a photon blaster," TJ said. "Duh."

"A photon blaster." Klyk considered the facts. "With that and his energy from eating, Mim will be hard for me to contain in my current state."

"Maybe we can reprogram the shrink ray to reverse itself and make you bigger. I can probably tweak the code."

"That's not a bad idea," Klyk said. "But we have to do it fast. Once Mim's appetite reaches critical mass, he could devour your whole planet in less than a day."

"Then we've got a lot of work to do," said Kevin. "Let's go."

Thin blades of sunlight shone through the slats in the blinds of the bunkhouse window as morning broke. Kevin squinted bleary-eyed as he woke up. Warner, Tara, and TJ were sprawled out in different places across the room. "Guys, wake up! We fell asleep!"

"Huh?" Tara's eyes popped open. "What time is it?"

"Quarter to seven," Kevin said. "TJ, we have to finish the program update."

"I already finished it," TJ grumbled, half-asleep. "I put the final touches on the program and loaded it onto the shrink ray before I passed out. What do you think I am, some kind of slacker?"

"Well, what are we waiting for?" Kevin said. "Let's go give it a test run!"

"Someone hit the snooze button on Kevin, will ya?" Warner said, still trying to get a few winks in. "Kevin, you can continue being super annoying five minutes from now."

TJ, still sleepy, raised his index finger at Kevin and said, "Boop."

Kevin took a breath and sank back down into his

pillow. "Wait," he said. "Where's Klyk?"

"I'm under the bed," said the miniaturized alien. "These weapons are useless!"

"What weapons?" Kevin dropped off the top bunk and looked under the bottom bed. He gasped at what he saw underneath.

Klyk had opened all of TJ's prized collection of action figures from their mint-condition packaging. He was fiddling with the little plastic toy gadgets. "These

devices are fakes. A cruel ruse!"

"OOOOH!" Kevin exclaimed, looking at the vintage toy packages torn asunder. "TJ's gonna be ticked!"

"What's TJ gonna be ticked about?" asked TJ, crawling across the floor to look under Kevin's bed. His bleary eyes squinted behind his glasses, and he squealed like a baby.

"What's he shrieking about?" Klyk asked Kevin as TJ hyperventilated.

"You just ripped open his favorite toys in the entire world, which would have been worth a lot of money one day if you hadn't done that," Kevin explained.

"These pieces of elementary junk?" Klyk held up a vintage action figure's tiny plastic accessory. "I thought these men were in cryostasis." The alien pointed to the lifeless toys lying in the shadows under the bed.

"Come on," said Kevin. "Let's get the supersizer ready for testing."

Warner placed his hand on TJ's shoulder, comforting his friend as he mourned the loss of his priceless plastic pals.

Tara flicked the light switch on her way over to the shrink ray, but nothing happened. She flipped it up and down a few more times, but the room remained dark. "I think the power's out."

"Yeah," said TJ, trying to get online with his laptop.

"There's no internet connection either."

Warner picked up his smartphone. "No cell service, either."

"Hey guys, check this out," Tara said, peering out the window. "Notice anything different?"

The boys gathered around and looked out across the camp. Almost everything was the same, except all the power lines were missing. Kevin couldn't even see the radio satellite tower that usually hovered in the distance.

Klyk strolled out from under the bed. "Mim," he said.

"He's cut off all our communication," said Tara.

"Well, at least we have the walkie-talkies," TJ said.

"Hey, what about Cody, Nick, and Bailey?" Kevin said, looking down at Klyk. "What was that stuff you guys were shooting with?"

"We call those cell blocks," said Klyk. "They'll be fine. That chemical substance is not lethal."

"How do we get them out?" Warner asked.

"You don't," said Klyk. "I do."

✿ ✿ ✿

When they reached the site of the previous night's camp-fire shootout, Kevin took Klyk out of his backpack and placed the mini alien in front of their three cell-blocked counselors. They watched Klyk place the palm of his hand on Bailey's transparent cocoon first, but nothing happened.

Klyk scratched his head in confusion. "It's supposed to know our handprints so when we want to release someone, we're the only ones who can. But it's not working." He tried again on Cody's and Nick's cocoons, only to get the same results. "Maybe it can't read my hands, they're so small."

"Time to get super-sized, Klyk," Kevin said, and placed him on a tree stump while TJ set up the new super-sizer on its tripod legs. Kevin took hold of the shrink ray and peered at the computer display. It looked almost as it did before, except now there was a new percentage scale on the screen to increase size. "Let's see," Kevin said. "You were about five times bigger before I shrank you, so we'll set the laser to five hundred percent."

"Ready," Kevin said, "aim . . . whoa!—stop!"

Out of the leafy bracken, Poobah, Mim's arachnopod, suddenly leaped between Klyk and the unshrink ray.

"Hold your fire!" Warner ordered TJ.

Tara trembled at the sight of the hybrid alien beast, which walked right up to the device and sniffed at it.

"Poobah," Kevin said. "No! Sit!"

Poobah looked up at Kevin and snarled, then gobbled up the alien gadget in one huge gulp.

"Noooo!" Kevin yelled.

The arachnopod glowed red from the inside out and then *ZAP!*—the wild arachnopod let out a squeal that almost busted Kevin's eardrums as it grew to five times its own size in an instant. Poobah's tentacles widened to the width of pillars, and its hairy spider legs were now as thick as tree trunks.

Klyk put his hand on his forehead and shook his head.

"At least we know it works," TJ said.

The size of a ranch house, the amphibious alien creature managed to squeeze nimbly between two large trees, squirming its way through the dense wooded terrain.

"Come on!" Kevin shouted, picking up Klyk off the tree stump and chasing after the extraterrestrial amphibian. "We have to get that shrink ray back."

"How? You just saw him eat it!" Warner said. "Are you insane?"

"I'm beginning to think so," Kevin said, and rushed off into the woods.

Poobah appeared again at the fringe of forest nearest the lake. Leaping off its massive spider legs, it bounded its way out of the woods and toward the mess hall. Poobah's tentacles flung up as it soared through the air and hacked off two huge tree branches, snapping them like they were twigs. It landed squarely on all eight of its appendages simultaneously. The earth trembled beneath its weight.

This is so not good, Kevin thought as he watched a group of campers and counselors make their way to the mess hall for breakfast.

Kevin sucked in a lungful of air as he watched the campers and remaining counselors swing their heads toward the tremor. It didn't take long before the first scream rang out.

Camp Director Dimpus looked up in horror at the massive arachnopod as campers shrieked and ran frantically for the mess hall. "Everyone inside!" he yelled. "Everyone inside!"

Kevin, Tara, TJ, and Warner sprinted out of the woods, merging into the onrush of campers hustling into the cafeteria.

Poobah stalked off the lakeside and onto the lawn, towering over one of the younger campers, who Kevin recognized was Bobby Little. Bobby stood in front of the ten-foot arachnopod, paralyzed with fear. The behemoth octo-spider craned its hideous face down at him and sniffed.

"Ahhhhh," Bobby screamed at the top of his lungs. He reached into his fanny pack and drew out two cans of OFF!, which he proceeded to spray in the beast's eyes.

Poobah reared back on its hindquarters and cast a broad shadow over Bobby Little.

Bobby tried to run, but one of the arachnopod's tentacles shot out and wrapped around Bobby's waist, lifting him up into the air. Bobby let out another high-pitched squeal, and Kevin rushed over to help his fellow camper.

"Poobah!" Kevin shouted at the humongous space creature. "Put him down!"

SQUAAWW! The arachnopod shrieked and threw Bobby to the grass. Bobby bounced back up to his feet and took off running for the mess hall, while Kevin stood face-to-face with the alien beast.

"Good Poobah," he said. "Nice Poobah."

The arachnopod's tentacle shot out again, straight for Kevin's head. Kevin leaped out of the way and ducked as one of the other tentacles came swiping for him.

"Run, Kevin!" Tara and Warner shouted from the mess hall. Kevin sprinted toward the entrance with Poobah on his heels, shooting globs of alien titanium silk at his ankles.

Once everyone was inside the cafeteria and safe under one roof, Dimpus slammed the door in Poobah's wretched spider face.

Kevin grabbed his knees, bent over at the waist, gasping for air.

"Do a head count!" Dimpus ordered, and the counselors started accounting for all the kids. Luckily, the entire camp had made it to breakfast on time except for Bailey, Cody, and Nick, who were still frozen out in the forest.

"See?" Alexander stomped forward after everyone had calmed down for a second. "I told you there were aliens!"

"Hey, settle down," said Tara's counselor, Marissa, as she came out of the back kitchen with a battery-operated radio. "We have a broadcast signal." She flipped it on and tuned it to the local news.

"In addition to multiple reports of large objects around the area inexplicably gone missing, an entire All-You-Can-Eat restaurant has just vanished," the local newscaster's voice reported.

"Mr. Brewer." Dimpus turned around to address Kevin. "Did you and your team have a hand in this?"

"I'd say a couple hands, sir," Alexander butted in.

"Kevin, what's going on here?" Dimpus said. "I want some answers!"

Well, Kevin thought. *I guess the arachnopod's out of the bag anyway.*

"It's true, sir." Kevin hung his head in shame. "We didn't invent a telepathy helmet. It came from outer space. We actually built a galactascope and made contact with an alien named Mim. We'd been hiding him in camp for the past few days, planning to bring him to the convention. But it turns out Mim's kind of a bad guy, so we need to stop him before he devours the, um, entire planet. Sorry."

"Say that again, Mr. Brewer," Dimpus said, his eyes wide with a mixture of surprise and disappointment.

Alexander stood up now, puffing out his chest. "A cheater in our midst. Shame on you, Kevo. Can't say that I'm all that surprised, though. I guess that makes me the winner, right, Dimpus? No offense to Team Quasar, but my hovercraft is way better than some soda that turns your hair purple."

Dimpus turned to them, looking even more flustered. "It was going to be the telepathy helmet, with the hovercraft as runner-up. But now that you've just confessed to cheating, Kevin, I guess the Vainglorious Math Nerds are indeed the winners of this year's convention."

"Yes!" Alexander pumped his fist and high-fived Luke and Dante.

"Umm, hey, nimrods," Tara interrupted. "There's kind of more important stuff going on here than the Invention Convention. . . . Like saving the world."

SQUAWW! The arachnopod let out another hideous

screech, which was followed by a loud thump that shook the mess hall as Poobah's giant tentacles slammed against the sides of the building. The windows started to crack, and another high-pitched twitter sounded from the alien beast.

"Counselors!" yelled Dimpus. "Barricade the entry points! Campers, remain calm!"

Strong, thick strands of arachnopod silk began looping around the building. The windows squeaked under the strain.

"What the heck's it doing?" Kevin opened his backpack and asked Klyk.

"It's cocooning us in," said Klyk. "We have to get

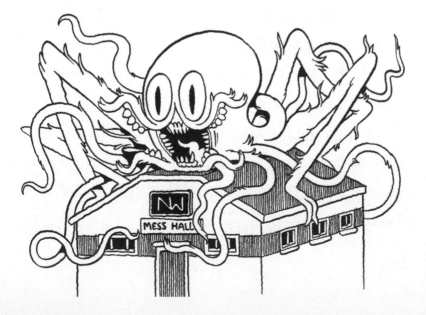

out of here. If we're trapped in here, we'll never be able to stop it."

As the counselors barricaded the doors, Kevin and the gang slipped out the back exit of the kitchen and climbed between the strands of arachnopod silk like the ropes on a pro wrestling ring.

"What about all the campers we've left behind?" Tara asked as the group made a mad dash for the boys' bunk, where their alien defense weaponry was stashed.

"Don't worry," Klyk insisted. "They'll be safer in there than out here with an arachnopod on the loose."

"So why are we outside, then?" Warner huffed and puffed.

"Because we're going to take this thing down." Kevin ran ahead of the pack.

As they burst through the door to their room, Kevin snatched up the bag holding the force-field gloves, the freeze ray, and the wormhole generator. He put on the gloves, then tossed the wormhole generator to Warner, and Tara took the freeze ray. "Hey!" said TJ. "What do I get?"

"You get to carry me," said Klyk. "Kevin, get ready. Everybody else fall in line."

"Here we go," Kevin whispered as they headed back outside and snuck around the corner of the cabin.

Kevin spied Poobah perched on top of the mess hall, finishing the cocoon-like web. The oversized beast jumped off the building, landing in the grass below, and Kevin and his teammates moved a little closer until Klyk ordered them to stop. They had a better angle now and Poobah hadn't spotted them, or so it seemed. "Take your best shot," Klyk said.

"With pleasure." Tara lined up the freeze ray on the unsuspecting arachnopod and hit the button. ZAP! A blue pulse of cryogenic plasma fired across the lawn directly toward the alien's midsection.

Poobah hopped straight up with the monstrous athleticism of a jumping spider. The blue laser landed on a tree trunk behind the arachnopod. The tree ceased swaying in the breeze, frozen by the pulse. Poobah touched back down in front of them and hissed a stream of sticky webbing straight at Kevin's face.

Kevin quickly brought the force-field gloves up to his face, bouncing the gelatinous web mucus straight back at Poobah's hideous maw. *YACK!* The massive arachnopod choked on the web at the back of its throat, and Tara fired off another blast.

The freeze ray vibrated and then blurped a dead battery sound. The blue pulse glowed faintly, and then the device shut down in Tara's hands. "It's out of juice!" she said, shaking the gadget.

"Guys, chill out," said Warner. "Let's just give him a taste of this baby." He patted the wormhole generator strapped to his wrist.

"And where would we send it?" Klyk asked. "There's not a cell in space prison big enough to hold it."

"You guys, we have to think of something," said Kevin. "It's our fault Poobah's even here."

"Kevin's right, we have to use our brains against this thing," said Tara. "It's bigger than us, but it's not smarter."

"Looks like we're going to have to do this the old-fashioned way," Warner said, already running straight for the sports shed. The rest of the group followed.

"Everybody in!" TJ shouted, holding the door open. Behind them, Poobah lurked low to the ground like a prowling cat, staring straight at them. Tara and Kevin scrambled into the shed as TJ pulled the door shut. Kevin set Klyk on the floor and dropped down to peer through the keyhole, but he couldn't get a visual. The arachnopod was out of his sight line.

"Did Mim say anything about the arachnopod?" Tara asked, searching through the shed for more tools that could bring Poobah down.

"Only that it's one of the only things in the universe that he can't eat," Kevin replied.

"That's right," said Warner. "You're a genius. The

arachnopod is allergic to Mim's fur, too."

"Hey, check it out," said Tara, wheeling over a caddy filled with tennis balls. "Mim's fur is all over these things!"

"You guys," said Warner. "I have an idea." He went to the back of the shed and rummaged around before he came back dragging a portable tennis ball shooter.

"Are you kidding me?" TJ said. "I was about to have that exact same idea."

"Okay, here's the plan," said Kevin, adjusting the power level on his force-field gloves. "Huddle up."

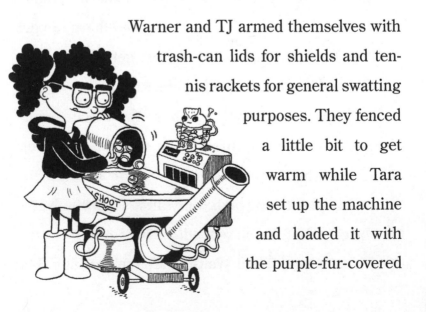

Warner and TJ armed themselves with trash-can lids for shields and tennis rackets for general swatting purposes. They fenced a little bit to get warm while Tara set up the machine and loaded it with the purple-fur-covered tennis balls. Klyk perched next to the controls on the tennis ball shooter.

Warner looked at Kevin, who was warming up with the force-field gloves. He then looked at his own make-shift weaponry. "Sure you don't want to trade?"

"I'm sure," Kevin said. "I'm just starting to get good with these things."

"Okay, ready," Tara said. "Let's do this before that thing starts to cocoon us."

The entire shed trembled as a loud thud shook the ground outside and Poobah's immense arachnopod tentacles came smashing through the windows.

"What did I tell you?" Tara screamed as they all dove for cover from the bear-hugging tentacles criss-crossing overhead. In an instant, Poobah pulled upward and the entire shed ripped out of its foundation.

"Charge!" Klyk shouted.

Kevin popped up and ran forward to face the mighty beast. Poobah reared back on its spider legs and simul-taneously jabbed two powerful tentacles at him. Kevin raised the force-field gloves to block the arachnopod's opening attack. Its tentacles flew back in response. Armed with their tennis rackets and metal shields, Warner and TJ helped Tara position the ball machine.

"Fire!" Klyk shouted, and Tara aimed the shooter right at the arachnopod's squawking maw.

PHLUMP-PHLUMP. The machine lobbed the first two tennis balls toward Poobah. The arachnopod's kryptonite arced through the air, but Poobah closed his mouth and both the tennis balls bounced off his brow in a puff of purple fur.

The revolting alien beast sucked in a torrent of air and then let out a dreadful sneeze, sending extraterrestrial snot everywhere. TJ stood there covered in slimy alien mucus and started to hyperventilate.

"Watch out!" Kevin hollered. "It's sneezing again."
He leaped to the side, hit the ground, and rolled clear of the splatter zone.

Warner and TJ lunged forward with their trash-can lids to shield themselves and Tara from the alien snot rockets flying through the air.

Poobah's last sneeze shook it to its very core, and its belly contracted. Kevin saw Poobah's stomach flash red as the supersizer shrink ray activated in its belly and sent out another laser beam.

ZAP! Poobah grew two times its already enormous stature. Now it stood halfway to the treetops, and its legs spanned the width of an entire professional soccer field.

"Aw, man," said Kevin to no one in particular.

"Seriously. That's a big arachnopod," TJ said.

"And a bigger target," said Klyk.

"You know the old saying," said Tara, lining up the

tennis ball shooter. "The bigger they are, the harder they fall."

THWAP-THWAP. Poobah shot two gobs of sticky spider silk through the air. Warner caught the first one with the trash-can lid, but the second gobbet nailed the shooting nozzle on the tennis ball machine.

"It's jammed!" Tara yelled, trying to send off another round.

Thinking quickly, Warner grabbed three tennis

balls, linty with Mim fur, and lobbed them one after the other with his racket. The trio of tennis balls sailed up into the air. The first two balls soared toward the beast's face, one hitting the arachnopod right in the eyeball, the second careening off the monster's slimy, foaming muzzle. But the third tennis ball was dead on and dropped straight into the arachnopod's mouth.

Instantly, Poobah's face bugged out, its panel of eyes bulging as it choked the tennis balls down into its digestive tract.

Tara and TJ both looked at Warner with amazement, and Kevin furrowed his brows at his pal.

"What?" asked Warner. "I thought you guys knew I played tennis." He spun the racket on his finger and blew imaginary smoke off the handle.

Within moments, Poobah started to wobble and its massive spider legs began to crumple under its own monstrous weight.

"Kevin, watch out!" Tara shouted as the supersized octo-spider toppled in his direction.

Kevin raised the force-field gloves to deflect the

falling creature, but as he thrust his hands up at the gigantic tentacle flopping down upon him, he felt the power from the gloves drain. *Uh-oh,* he thought. He may as well have been wearing the ugly green mittens his grandma had knitted him for his birthday.

"**O**omph!" Kevin's body struck the ground, and he landed flat on his rear, the back of his head slamming into the grass. Beams of sunlight shone through the dust cloud, and Kevin coughed. He couldn't move. His legs were trapped beneath the arachnopod's gargantuan tentacle. "Help!" he called. "I'm stuck!"

Tara and TJ rushed over and grabbed him by the arms, trying to yank him out from under Poobah's hefty weight.

"Kevin, are you okay?" Tara asked.

"Except for being trapped under a giant arachnopod, I think I'm fine."

Tara and TJ tried to lift the tentacle, but straining with both hands, they could only lift it about an inch and a half.

"It's slippery!" TJ moaned.

They lifted again with all their might as Warner came over and yanked both of Kevin's arms by the wrist.

"Easy, man." Kevin grimaced. "You're gonna dislocate my shoulders!"

"Almost there, buddy!" Warner said, straining to pull Kevin free. "One, two, three!"

Kevin felt himself lurch upward as his legs dislodged from under the weight of Poobah's octo-arm. Warner dragged Kevin a few feet away from the monstrous arachnopod and set his friend down.

"Just gimme a sec," Kevin said, stretching his arms and legs. When he was ready, Kevin rose to his feet and brushed himself off next to his friends. The four of them stood gazing at the fallen arachnopod. Except for its slow, shallow breathing, Poobah was completely still.

"It's not looking so good," Kevin said.

"It must be really allergic to Mim," said TJ.

With a jolt, Poobah began to hiccup. Quickly, the hiccup fit turned into an awful spell of dry heaving.

"You guys might want to stand back," said Klyk.

PHFLU-ARGH! Out sprayed a wave of extraterrestrial bile as the amphibious mutant got sick, over and over. *PHLU-ARGH!*

The alien throw-up doused the front of Tara's shirt. "Ick!" she squealed, and backed away as more upchuck spilled from the octo-spider's mouth.

"Nasty!" Warner said with a little amusement in his voice.

The arachnopod gagged and coughed once more,

and with a final gurgle, the supersizer ray shot out of Poobah's mouth and landed at Kevin's feet.

Kevin bent down and picked up the device, wiping it off on his shorts. When he opened the screen, the monitor lit up. "It's still working," he said.

"No duh," said TJ, gesturing to the gigantic arachnopod lying before them.

"Thank goodness," said Tara. "We've been wasting too much time on Poobah. We have to get Mim before he destroys the whole world! What are we gonna do?"

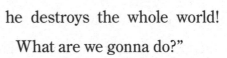

Kevin thought hard, but he was out of ideas.

"Wait, you guys," Tara said. "Where's the galactascope?"

"It's in the gym in the field house," Kevin said. "We left it there after the Invention Convention."

"Okay, well, why don't we

go use that to call Klyk's alien backup?"

"I can't believe we didn't think of that already!" Kevin shouted, and they all took off for the field house.

But when they reached the gymnasium, their proud invention was no longer where they'd left it. "Mim!" Kevin growled, tightening his fist into a ball. "He must have taken it to cut us off."

"What are we going to do, you guys?" TJ asked a little meekly. "I don't want our planet to get eaten up by that little scuzzball."

"Me neither," Tara said, and they all fell quiet for a long moment.

Finally Klyk broke the silence. "If we can get within shooting distance of the little sucker, then we can zap him back to the intake facility on my planet's prison system."

"Okay, then let's unshrink Klyk so he can track down Mim and wormhole the crud out of him," Warner said.

"I wish it were that easy," said Klyk.

"What are you saying?"

"Mim gets stronger and quicker from his feedings, which makes him harder to catch and contain. If the news we heard earlier is right, he might already be unstoppable."

"But you're a highly trained intergalactic crime fighter," Warner blurted. "You're our best shot. We've got to make you big again."

"How much juice do we have left?" Kevin asked.

"Seven percent," said TJ. "One shot."

They pondered the dilemma in the morning silence.

There's got to be another way, thought Kevin.

"So if we don't do something now, he'll just keep eating more and more?" Tara asked.

"That's right," said Klyk. "And then he'll eat some more."

A lightbulb flashed in Kevin's brain. "S'more," he said.

"That's what he just said, man," Warner said.

"No," said Kevin. "Suh-mores," he annunciated the word more precisely. "Mim's new favorite food!" He turned to Klyk. "Sorry, man, we can't unshrink you. Not yet, anyway."

"Wait," said Tara. "Why?"

"Because we're gonna use our one shot to lure Mim back to us with the biggest s'more ever and then zap him out of this world!"

"It might work," said Klyk. "But I'm warning you, if we do find him, this won't be the Mim you know. Mim's gastrointestinal anatomy is such that everything that enters his mouth will be converted into pure energy, which he uses to feed on more matter. Mim is like a micro black hole of mass consumption."

"Then we're going to have to execute this operation to perfection," said Kevin. "Are you with me?"

"Yeah!" the four of them all shouted, and then sprang into action.

Kevin and Warner dashed back to the bunkhouse to gather up the last of Warner's graham cracker, marshmallow, and chocolate bar supply.

When they returned, Tara and TJ had a bonfire all ready to concoct the biggest s'more of all time.

Once they had roasted all the marshmallows and

used up the rest of the graham crackers and chocolate, they moved the s'more to the center of the field at the back of camp.

"Make it count, Kev," said Warner. "This is our only shot."

Kevin lined up the alien gadget and set the size-o-meter as high as it would go. He tapped the touch screen, sending a laser beam blasting out into the field.

With expert precision, the beam zapped the s'more, and the Extraordinary Terrestrials watched the delicious treat grow to the size of a basketball court. The surrounding area filled with the sweet-smelling aroma of melted chocolate and gooey marshmallow.

"Nice job," Klyk declared behind them as the four kids all high-fived.

Kevin spun around and saw Klyk dragging something through the grass. It was Alexander's miniaturized hovercraft from the gymnasium.

"I thought this could be of use in catching Mim. I made some modifications to this vehicle. The engine will run silently now," Klyk said. "But I was unable to access the ignition. There seems to be some kind of secret pass code."

"Hold on a sec," Kevin said. "I'll handle this."

He rushed across campus and back to the mess hall, where the campers were still cocooned inside. "Alexander!" Kevin called through the layers of alien silk surrounding the building.

After a brief pause, Alexander's voice could be heard coming from inside. "What is it?"

"What's the password for your hovercraft?"

"That's for me to know and you to find out," Alexander said.

"Come on, this is serious. Just tell me the code."

"Not until you admit that you're an alien."

"I'm not an alien," Kevin said.

"You are if you want the pass code," Alexander said.

"Fine," said Kevin. "I'm an alien. Happy now?"

"Say it like you mean it," Alexander said.

"Give me the code, man!" Kevin shouted.

"Alexander!" Dimpus's voice boomed from within. "Give Kevin the code already! Our lives depend on it."

"Easy peasy one two threesy," Alexander said.

"I'm waiting . . . ," Kevin said.

"That's the code, you nimrod," Alexander said.

"Thanks!" Kevin darted back to the group, saying the code over and over to himself. "EZPZ123Z."

"Klyk, I got it!" Kevin shouted to the little alien, who was sitting on Warner's arm. He was setting the coordinates for the wormhole generator to send Mim to his specially designed prison cell made out of arachnopod silk— the only thing he couldn't eat his way out of—halfway across the galaxy.

"Phew!" Tara said as a low rumble resounded in the distance. "I think Mim's coming!"

Klyk punched in the code, and the hovercraft engine purred to life. The mini alien cyborg hopped in and flew over to the unconscious arachnopod and yanked out a long stretch of the alien beast's silk from the gland on one of its tentacles. He tied it securely to the back of the hovercraft, then rode behind a bush and disappeared from view.

Warner, Tara, TJ, and Kevin all darted away from the gigantic s'more and into the forest to await their alien friend turned foe. Less than twenty seconds later, nearby trees began to disappear off the horizon and before long, a huge path the width of a highway started to clear seemingly on its own. Entire trees were being chewed up like they were branches in a wood chipper.

At the center of the mass consumption, Mim levitated off the ground, his mouth a chaotic vortex of churning dark energy.

Mim stopped before the megasized s'more. He had a frenzied look in each of his four eyes.

"Mim," said Tara, stepping out nervously with Kevin and TJ by her side. "We offer you . . . an offering!"

"Yeah," TJ chimed in. "I reversed the shrink ray to make gigantic things for you to eat. Wasn't that nice of me?"

"That was very thoughtful, TJ," said Mim.

"Mim," said Kevin. "We've done nothing but try to help you since you arrived here. We want you to feel at home, so we made this gigantic s'more specially for you."

"How do I know it's not poisoned?" Mim asked. "You eat it first."

"Okay," Kevin said, and walked over to take a handful of the melted chocolate and marshmallow. "Yum," he said, eating a big gob out of his bare hand.

Tara and TJ took handfuls of the s'more, too, and started eating them. "Mmm," Tara said. "It's sooooo good."

"That's enough," Mim said, his stomach grumbling audibly. "The rest is mine!"

Strands of alien drool windmilled off its black hole of a mouth as Mim began to suck down the rest of the megasized s'more.

With Mim distracted, Klyk came zooming out from his hiding spot in the woods, riding the souped-up mini hovercraft, and began to lasso lengths of superstrong arachnopod silk between Mim's legs.

"What's this?" Mim roared, and swatted the hovercraft to the ground. Klyk flew out of the control seat and bounced hard twice in the dirt before rolling to a stop.

"Wait. Can it really be?" Mim asked, standing over

the fallen alien soldier. "Klyk . . . but you are so tiny!" The psychotic purple fluffball let out a deep, bellowing laugh that seemed to echo off itself. One of Mim's arms stretched elastically down and plucked Klyk off the ground. Klyk dangled limply in his grip before Mim dropped his miniaturized foe to the grass and turned to the kids.

"You filthy little sneaks!" Mim howled. "You think you can trick Mim? Mim *is* the trickster!"

"Uh-oh, guys," said Tara. "He's talking about himself in the third person. That can't be good."

"Just you wait!" yelled Kevin. "Warner, now!"

Warner jumped out of hiding and clicked the button on the generator, but nothing happened.

"Warner!" they all yelled.

"Sorry, sorry," he said. "I was trying to save power. I forgot to turn it back on!"

Two of Mim's eyes rotated and landed their gaze on Warner aiming the wormhole generator.

"Come on, come on, hurry!" TJ yelled.

But before Warner could hit the button, Mim leaped

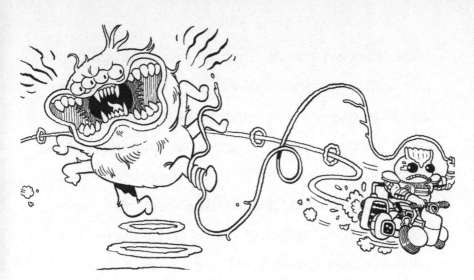

away from the kids and shot up high in the air.

As the furious fur ball levitated to the treetops, the arachnopod silk tightened in a knot around one of his ankles. "Growrghk—" Mim yowled. Tethered by the thread of arachnopod silk, the purple planet eater wriggled above their heads like an airborne kite tugging at the end of its line.

Mim pulled the de-atomizer ray from his fur. He flicked it on, preparing to cut himself loose.

Ping! The wormhole generator reloaded and Warner took aim, firing the one and only shot they had to save mankind.

ZWHOOSH! The wormhole blast shot out just as

Mim triggered the de-atomizer ray and zapped the arachnopod silk free from his legs. The line snapped and Mim floated twenty feet in the air. Yet before he could escape, a portal of green shimmering plasma opened up and sucked the all-consuming alien fiend into its vacuum. Mim fought against the wormhole's suction, but his powerful vortex of matter-craving energy was not enough to escape the pull. In the blink of an eye, the wormhole closed and sent a shock wave that knocked them all backward.

"Whoa," said TJ as he stood up and then helped Kevin and Tara off the ground.

"I did it!" Warner leaped for joy, thrusting the wormhole generator into the air. "I mean, *we* did it."

"Klyk!" Kevin shouted, and ran over to where Mim had swatted the hovercraft to the ground.

The mini hovercraft was beyond repair, and Klyk was lying perfectly still in the grass.

"Is he . . . ?" TJ asked.

"I don't know," Kevin said, shaking the alien softly. "Klyk?"

The miniaturized alien cyborg's eyes flickered open, and he sat up. "What happened?"

"We got him!" the four campers cheered, and started high-fiving each other again.

Then Kevin offered his pinkie finger to their pint-size alien friend, and he high-fived it, too. Klyk let out a mighty yelp and raised his tiny arm in victory. "Mission accomplished."

As the group continued their celebratory dance around the campground, Kevin glanced at the mess hall, which was entirely cocooned in Poobah's silk. "How are we supposed to get everyone out of there?"

"Get the de-atomizer," TJ said. "Mim dropped it before he got wormholed."

They ran to the spot below where Mim had been sucked out of the sky and found the small dumbbell-shaped device in the grass. Kevin picked it up and ran over to the mess hall.

"Good news, everyone!" Kevin shouted through the cocoon. "We're about to get you guys out of here."

The camp cheered and then quieted down.

"Kevin, is it safe out there?" Dimpus asked.

"Yes, sir," Kevin said. "I think we pulled through."

"May I do the honors?" TJ asked Kevin.

"Here." Klyk stopped TJ for a moment and showed him how to turn off the blast setting and turn the de-atomizer into a laser-cutting tool.

"Cool," TJ said, and stood ready to cut through the cocoon. "Everybody stand back!"

The red-hot laser beam sizzled through the arach-nopod silk as TJ cut a hole through the cocoon to the actual door.

The campers slowly filed out of the mess hall and gasped at the now even bigger arachnopod lying conked out on the ground.

"What are we going to do with that thing?" Dimpus slapped his forehead. "It's huge!"

"Has anyone seen Cody, Nick, or Bailey?" Tara's counselor, Marissa, asked.

"Oh yeah," said Kevin. "They got trapped in these alien cocoon things."

"But they're all good," Warner said. "Don't worry. We'll get them back to normal soon."

"Oh," she said, a bit bewildered. "Okay . . ."

"Let's hear it for Kevin and the Extraordinary Terrestrials!" little Bobby Little shouted at the top of his lungs.

"Hip hip hooray!" they all cheered, picking Kevin, Warner, and Tara up onto their shoulders. Kevin looked around for TJ but couldn't spot his once-silent buddy anywhere. "Hip hip hooray!"

Once their fellow campers put Kevin, Tara, and Warner back on the ground, Dimpus and the rest of the counselors attempted to regain control of the camp. Suddenly a hand tapped Kevin on the arm and pulled him away from the pandemonium.

"Hey, there you are, Teej!" Kevin said, turning around. "I was looking for you. You missed—" But he stopped short, seeing the panic on his friend's face. "What's up?"

TJ's eyes were bugging out, and he kept trying to say a million things at once. "You're not gonna—I don't know—the galactascope—I found—come on!"

Behind the observatory building, their galactascope was pointed toward the bright-blue afternoon sky. Klyk hopped out of his bag, and Kevin set the little alien down on top of the machine.

Onscreen, the instant messenger menu was already open, frozen on a message written in a strange language.

"What is that?" Kevin said to Klyk. "Do you know what it says?"

TJ hit the translate function, and they all squinted

at the computer monitor. "THE FEAST ENDS TODAY. THE TAKEOVER STARTS TOMORROW."

"Wait," said Klyk. "There's a return message from Z&N777. It says: 'On our way.'"

"Who's on their way?" Warner asked.

"I'm not exactly sure whose alias this is." Klyk scratched his head. "Mim runs with a pretty rough crowd. It could be any number of his associates."

"They're on their way here?" Kevin asked, a tight, sick feeling brewing in his stomach.

"Come on, then," Tara said. "We have to contact your planet and tell them we need reinforcements."

They aimed the galactascope's satellite dish up at the sky. Klyk typed a new message to his commanding officer and hit send, but the message wouldn't transmit.

"What's going on?" Klyk said. "It's not working!"

"Uh-oh," TJ said, inspecting the wire hookup. "Mim must have snipped a bunch of these wires after he received his response. I can probably fix it in a few hours, but I don't think we have hours." TJ pointed to the sky, and they all turned to look.

The clouds overhead roiled furiously as a fleet of four UFOs descended over the camp.

"Uh-oh," TJ said.

"Is that—?" asked Warner.

"Whoever that is," Klyk said, gasping a bit. "I doubt they've come in peace."

As Kevin stood with his friends looking up at the alien spaceships, he felt his nervous stomach begin to churn again, but he wasn't scared. He'd brought Mim here and he'd sent him back, and he was going to do the same to Mim's partners in space crime. So what if he and his friends didn't win the Invention Convention or the trip to Hawaii? If they didn't come up with a good plan soon, there might not be any more Hawaii, or anywhere else for that matter. Kevin looked over at Warner, TJ, and Tara.

"Put on your thinking caps, guys," he said. "Time to brainstorm."

ACKNOWLEDGMENTS

Many thanks to my editor, Emilia Rhodes, for guiding me safely through the alien underworld; to Josh Bank and Sara Shandler for their otherworldly brainstorming skills; to Rachel Abrams for her extraterrestrial attention to detail; and to Ryan Harbage for keeping peace throughout the galaxy.

JOHN KLOEPFER is the author of the popular undead series The Zombie Chasers. He is currently unzombified and figuring out ways to stop aliens from taking over the planet. He lives in New York City.

NICK EDWARDS is a cartoonist, illustrator, and character designer from London, UK. He earned his illustration degree at Brighton University. Nick's work can be seen on Cartoon Network and the Disney Channel, as well as in *Dinopopolous,* his first comic with Blank Slate Books.

THE ACTION CONTINUES IN

Into the Dorkness

Kevin Brewer and his best friends, Warner, Tara, and TJ, are having the best—and the worst—summer ever. After accidentally summoning one of the galaxy's most wanted alien criminals to their science camp, they blasted the intergalactic bad guy back into outer space and saved the world.

For a nanosecond, Kevin is king of the universe. But then a new alien criminal duo invades Earth, bringing an army of extraterrestrial bees with brainwashing stingers. Buzzkill!

Kevin and his buddies must gear up to save the world—again. But it will take a stroke of genius to outsmart these alien cons. Will the Extraordinary Terrestrials be up to the task?